LOVESOM

Chapter One

It was raining when Ruth Kendal came back to Derham; a fine summer rain that misted the windscreen of her car, obliterating the familiar panorama of the dale for a moment before she started the wipers to clear her vision of the homeland scene. If she had come back to Skeldale for good that was the way it had to be, she thought. She had no regrets. The job she had left behind her in London had been a good one, satisfying in every respect, but the fate of Lovesome Hill farm was paramount on her mind. Her mother needed her now as never before.

She drove down the hill and across the ford where the brown water slid gently over the road and up on the other side, remembering how they had played there as children – Becky and she and the brother they had both adored. Jonathan had gone now, dismissed from the family by a harsh parent who had considered individuality a crime. George Kendal had been a harsh taskmaster, expecting them all to conform to his rigid code of conduct, and his daughters had not disappointed him. Ruth had succeeded in London while Becky was in her first year at York University, studying geology, and he had died a fairly contented man. His wife, Hester, a strong woman, had taken on the running of the farm on her husband's death, determined to keep her son's inheritance intact although, in her heart of hearts, she feared that he was dead. They had had no news of Jonathan for three years. He had quarrelled with his father four years ago over his desire to spend a year back-packing in Australia and George Kendal had told him not to come back if he persisted in going abroad.

After a year Jonathan's letters to his mother had ceased and, although Hester kept a stiff upper lip and got on with her busy life at Lovesome Hill, Ruth knew that her mother had never stopped grieving for her only son. She also knew that Hester would work herself into the ground rather than take Becky away from university. In that respect she was as full of pride as her late husband had been, but recently her health had suffered as the result of a slight stroke which had put her in bed for over a month. It was the reason for Ruth's return to her birthplace and, as she drove up through the trees which sheltered Skeldale beck and reached the brow of the hill, she determined to put the past firmly behind her. Before her lay the future whatever that might bring.

Coming out of the shadow of the trees the sun blinded her for a moment and then she was able to look down on the full beauty of the dale which lay beneath her. A light mantle of mist made the moorland all the more remote, but beneath it she could see the early summer fields criss-crossed by the dry-stone walls which characterized all the dales as they rose to the brows of the distant hills. Skeldale was narrow and long, dominated by the towering bulk of the Scar, and down at its heart Derham lay quietly exposed to the sun. The scattering of houses were all familiar to her as she traced the path of the meandering river and picked out the grey ribbon of the road winding beside it.

Her eyes rose to the distant hills and suddenly there was a rainbow forming half an arch ahead of her. There was no end to it that she could see, but her heart was lifted and she drove on with more enthusiasm than she had felt for some time.

The road she followed was still high and presently she became aware of change. She had reached High Parks, a remote property which had remained deserted for many years since the previous owner had died, but now the wall that surrounded it had been recently repaired. New stone had been worked into the old, new trees had been planted within the perimiter wall.

Curiously she slowed down into second gear. Someone had built that wall, a brash new stone barrier that stuck out like a sore thumb against the mellowed landscape of green fields and ancient trees and the village she loved nestling in the narrow dale beneath them.

When she finally reached the entrance to High Parks, itself new, wrought-iron gates were firmly closed against any possible intrusion, but what compelled her interest most was the twin stone birds poised on the pillars on either side of the gates. The Stone Birds! Nobody in the Dale had ever been sure what kind of bird they were supposed to represent – eagle or phoenix or some other mystical creature born of a sculptor's frenzied imagination, poised there gazing at the world through lidless eyes. A long time ago – long before Ruth was born – they had been a feature of the estate and an odd legend had grown up around them. If they ever fell from their stony perch the Jeffs or their successors would be dogged by dire misfortune until the day they died. Shortly before Bob Jeffs had been killed in an accident a storm had demolished the original wall and the Stone Birds had been buried under it. Grass and weeds had grown over them and they had been forgotten.

That had been a long time ago, Ruth thought, and she had almost forgotten about it, but now it all came rushing back to her as if to draw her into its evil spell. Bob Jeffs must have died over twenty years ago but his ill-fated story had lingered on in the dale and High Parks had remained empty ever since. It must be almost a ruin by now, she reflected, standing there on the edge of the moor where the winds blew strongest and the snow came early to blanket the land in pristine white. It had been years since she had heard of the legend, but now the details came vividly to mind, whispered in awe between two sisters when they spoke about something they did not understand. Becky had been the dramatic one, she thought, while she had been more like her practical mother. Hester Kendal had brushed 'such nonsense' aside whenever they had questioned her, but the legend had held a fascination for them which they had been unable to disguise.

"Do you suppose there might be a ghost up there?" Becky had never tired of asking in those far-off childhood days. "Old man Jeffs coming back to haunt the place, trying to keep it for himself in spite of the Stone Birds?"

Ruth had said stoutly that she didn't believe in ghosts, mostly to reassure her younger sister, but quite often the legend of the Stone Birds had recurred to her, making her wonder about them. Then, when she had gone to London to take up a lucrative post as secretary in a large advertising firm she had forgotten all about them, as no doubt the dale had done in its turn.

Here they were, however, raised again and glaring down at her as she pulled up to take a second look at them. Whatever creature they were supposed to represent, she mused, they succeeded in suggesting evil and their weathered ugliness was certainly not in keeping with the brave new wall.

She sat for a moment weighing them up until two dogs came barking towards her, one of them a red setter who jumped up against her off-side door.

"Down, Rufus! Do as you are told."

The man's autocratic command came sharply through

her half-open window, contrasting with the silence all around her, but before she could let in her clutch to drive away a tall stranger in a waterproof jacket with cord trousers thrust into green Wellington boots and a cloth cap drawn firmly down over his eyes blocked her view. He had been out in the rain for some time it seemed, walking on the moor, and she had the distinct impression that he had enjoyed his battle with the elements.

"I'm sorry," she apologized, feeling for the gear leaver. "Am I blocking your way?"

Fierce blue-grey eyes met hers from under the cloth cap.

"I'm capable of vaulting a wall," the man informed her briefly. "I thought you might be in trouble with your car."

"No – not really," she answered. "I was looking at the Stone Birds. I haven't seen them before – only heard about them."

A thin, barely amused smile spread over his deeply tanned face.

"You mean the legend, of course," he said, his firm lips twisting. "Interesting in its own way but utterly ridiculous. That's why I had them put back there," he added. "I also re-built the wall."

"You've bought High Parks?" Her tone was almost incredulous.

"Why not?" he demanded.

"Because it's been empty for so long," Ruth found herself saying. "It must be years since Bob Jeffs was killed."

"Twenty, to be exact," he said. "Accidents happen."

She tried to laugh. "I don't think I've ever blamed the Stone Birds for Bob's death!"

"Yet you're inclined to believe in the legend," he suggested with fine scorn.

5

She shrugged. "Not too strongly. I'm a modern miss, I suppose," Ruth declared, letting in her clutch. "I'm on my way home," she added for his further enlightenment, supposing that they might have to meet again.

He looked down at Derham with a speculative eye, but he did not ask her where home might be.

When Ruth finally arrived at Lovesome Hill farm her sister was already there. Becky had been watching for her all morning, chafing at what she considered her sister's slow progress after she had left the A1 near Northallerton to make the final part of her journey home.

"I thought you'd never get here," she remonstrated, restraining the two welcoming sheep-dogs who had bounded towards the car. "What kept you so long?"

"An ageing car and the delight of coming home!"

Ruth was out of the car now, folding her younger sister in a fond embrace. Becky had changed. She was still the beauty of the family, a lovely, attractive blonde, strong-willed like her brother and quite unable to understand Ruth's anxiety about the future.

"You had no need to give up your job," she said bluntly, "especially when you were making such a success of it. We could have managed."

"How?" Ruth asked, unloading some of her luggage from the back seat. "You can't run a farm from an invalid chair."

"Mother's trying to walk with a stick now. We'll get someone in." Becky stood beside the car, not offering to help with the rest of the luggage. "It was bad luck Amos Farley hurting his back like that, but Mother will cope. She always has."

Until now, Ruth thought, refusing an argument as she looked beyond Becky at the solid old stone farmhouse, surrounded by the high stone barns where they had played as children, where they had all been born. To the unseeing eye it might have appeared bleak with its stepped gables and grey weathered slates and tall chimneys reaching for the sky, but it held a world of memories for them both.

"Mother's inside," Becky informed her. "She finds the steps difficult."

"We'll get a ramp fixed," Ruth suggested. "She'll want to get out into the fresh air as much as possible. She loves her garden." She turned on her heel. "Can you bring my anorak and the handbag on the front seat? They're not heavy."

Becky delved into the car as Ruth turned towards the house where the side door had been left open for her. Two shallow stone steps led up to the entrance where Hester Kendal was waiting and Ruth was instantly aware of her mother's vulnerability, her natural strength sapped by anxiety and the physical exhaustion of her recent illness.

"You've come!" Hester said, not trying to hide her relief. "We've been waiting for you all morning."

"So Becky has been telling me." Ruth hugged her mother tightly. "Now, I'm here and you can kill the fatted calf! I'm not likely to go back to London for a very long time."

For a moment longer Hester clung to her hand. Not easily given to demonstrations of affection, she was anything but a hard woman and her dark eyes betrayed her gratitude.

"It will only be for a week or two," she promised, "till Amos is back on his feet again. He's slow, of course, because of his back, but he's doing the best he can."

"Does this mean he'll want to retire, at last?" Ruth asked, following her along the short passageway to the front hall.

"He's seventy-four," Hester reminded her.

7

"I'd forgotten," Ruth admitted, noticing how heavily her mother depended on the stout stick she carried. "We'll talk about more help right away."

Becky followed them into a sitting-room made bright by a glowing log fire in a wide grate in an ingle nook. It was a family place where they had sat so often in the past, their father in his slippers after a hard day's work on the land and Hester, always with some knitting in her hands, never idle even when she came through from the stone-flagged kitchen where she had prepared their evening meal. Now she turned eagerly to look at both her daughters.

"It's like old times," she said bravely, trying to hide the shadow in her eyes.

Ruth sat down in her father's chair.

"What's been happening," she asked, "apart from Amos hurting his back?"

"Not a lot," Becky was quick to inform her. "I'm still riding as much as I can on other people's horses when I'm at home and there's the usual flurry of excitement in Derham at the prospect of summer visitors. Even the Metcalfs have rented out one of their houses this year, although they needn't. Kate says it keeps the property aired, although she isn't keen on renting. They don't have to, of course. They've got everything they could ever want."

"Except contentment," Hester suggested from her arm-chair on the other side of the room. "I wouldn't like to be in Mrs Metcalf's expensive shoes. She hardly sees that man of hers unless he's stopping by for a meal on his way to some new ploy or other to further his business interests. They're good enough friends, I'll grant you, but to my way of thinking they're missing out on the true meaning of family life."

"It's nice knowing them, all the same," Becky declared.

8

"They give the best parties in the dale and Kate is always generous with her horses."

They had known the Metcalfs all their lives, two families living close enough to share a common interest in the dale, although the Metcalfs had succeeded spectacularly in business while the Kendals had continued to till the land.

"I've asked Kate to come to York occasionally but she doesn't feel inclined. Maybe she thinks she'd be out of her depth among a lot of rowdy undergraduates or maybe she just feels happy enough the way she is. Horses are all she really cares about."

"You don't really know that," Ruth said. "Kate does a lot of good in her own quiet way. Always has done," she added thoughtfully. "Especially with children."

"Teaching them to ride," Becky speculated. "I could do that."

"You've enough to do with your university work," Hester pointed out. "Stick in at that while you have the chance and think about horses later."

Becky took a restless turn about the room.

"I can't help thinking there's more to life than what I'm doing," she decided rebelliously. "Where is all this learning going to get me in the end?"

Ruth looked at her over their mother's head, her eyes sharp with concern. "To a purposeful job, we hope," she suggested.

"Oh, that!" Becky exclaimed, tossing her head. "That could be light years away." She stood beside the window for a moment, contemplating the outside scene like a small, restless animal confined by a constricting rein. "The worst part of learning is being indoors most of the time," she declared.

"Geology isn't exactly an indoors pursuit," Ruth reminded her. "You'll be out and about most of the time, I should imagine, and look at the scope you have up here in the Dales."

"I've been telling her that," Hester said. "It's an outdoor life whichever way you look at it."

All her own life she had worked in the open air, never tiring, always content to be close to nature and the contentment part of it was what she wanted most for her family, but already she had seen her only son driven away from his rightful inheritance on the land by an old man's anger and she feared for her youngest child.

"I'm going out," Becky announced, hitching up her blue jeans. "I've got a chance to ride. Kate Metcalf promised to lend me a horse."

"What about Jet?" Ruth asked.

"I've grown out of Jet." Becky looked impatient. "He's only a pony and I'll have to sell him eventually."

Ruth looked quickly away from her mother's disappointed eyes. "What about dinner?" she asked.

"Oh, I'll get something when I come back," Becky answered airily. "I'm not too keen on a heavy meal, anyway. I have to watch my figure. Everybody's on a diet at the hostel these days and I can't afford to be different. Besides, if I want to ride successfully I have to consider my weight."

"What did she mean about riding successfully?" Ruth asked when the door had closed behind her energetic sister. "She can't ride a horse around York."

Hester sighed. "I suppose she means when she is here occasionally," she suggested. "I've never felt that she was properly settled in York."

"It's what she wanted to do, wasn't it?" Ruth asked "She can't go chopping and changing at this stage."

"No," Hester said without conviction. "She's horse mad, of course. Always was."

"It's a hobby – nothing more," Ruth decided. "Maybe

it will bring her home more often, especially during the better weather."

"She has made a lot of new friends in York," Hester said. "I want her to be happy."

"She has every chance." Ruth turned to go to the kitchen to prepare some tea for them both. "She ought to be content."

"How about you?" her mother asked unexpectedly. "This is tearing up your life, coming home like this to look after me. You were doing so well in London."

"Well enough," Ruth had to admit, stopping at the door, "but I'm glad to be home now. Don't worry yourself about me, Mother," she added as she went out. "I'm happy to be here."

"It's not where you belong." Hester had hobbled behind her into the stone-flagged kitchen. "It's not what we had planned for you."

"'The best laid plans o' mice an' men'," Ruth quoted, turning to her with a smile. "I've made my decision and I mean to stay."

When she had infused the tea she found a tray and carried it back to the sitting-room where Hester was replenishing the fire.

"We've enough wood to last us a lifetime," her mother remarked. "A tree fell down in that last storm we had and Amos cut it up for firewood before he hurt his back. We'll manage," she ended optimistically. "We always have."

Ruth wanted to ask her about the future, just how they would manage, but decided that this was hardly the right time to do so.

"We're not all that strapped for cash," Hester assured her. "Your father had a tidy bit put away in the bank before he died. It's the question of help that doesn't come easy these days when young men don't take to farming as they did, especially in the Dales. It's too remote here for the

11

average youth unless he was born into farming and it's no job for a girl."

"Girls manage," Ruth assured her. "Women always have."

They drank the tea, sitting side by side in the easy intimacy of the ingle nook discussing the changes that had taken place since Ruth's last visit.

"Winterside Grange has been sold," her mother told her. "We haven't seen hilt nor hare of the new owner yet, but some say she's a widow woman with a child. A bit of a mystery, if you ask me, her not wanting to mix with the locals. Happen we're misjudging her, though," she added carefully. "She might just be taking longer to settle in than most."

"It's a big house for a woman and one child," Ruth suggested.

"Maybe she'll start entertaining come the winter," Hester said. "She must have a lot of sorting out to do."

"She seems to have brought her own help with her," Hester added, "so she must have money. Rumour has it that she dotes on the boy and won't let him out of her sight. Nobody seems to have seen much of the lad, as far as I can gather, and he's certainly not at the school. She's called Falconer, I hear, and Amos says she's a beauty. He saw her once in Derham when she first arrived, but that was weeks ago. Since then she seems to have shut herself up at the Grange without any contact with the dale at all."

"There seems to have been a lot of changes recently," Ruth mused. "Strangers to the dale who have only recently settled in."

Her thoughts flew back to her meeting with the man on the moor road on her way home.

"You didn't tell me about High Parks when you wrote," she prompted. "We have a new neighbour up there, too, I see."

12

Hester looked up in surprise. "You've met him?"

"I think I stumbled across him when I pulled up at the new gates to look at the Stone Birds," Ruth explained, "but we didn't get as far as an introduction before I drove on."

"His name's Bradley – Mark Bradley," Hester informed her. "He's an industrialist of some sort from the other side of the Pennines. Or so I'm told. I don't hold much with gossip, as you know, but Amos says he's turned High Parks upside down, meaning to breed horses or some such thing. He's employed a lad or two from the village already, but nobody seems to know too much about him so far."

"He may be some sort of recluse," Ruth offered, remembering her encounter on the moor road and the indifference in the man's eyes. Deep-set intensely blue eyes that could turn grey in a moment when he had ceased to be interested, eyes which she had found difficult to forget.

The subject of Winterside's new occupant and Mark Bradley forgotten, they ate their midday meal in the cosy atmosphere of the farmhouse kitchen where an Aga sent out its comforting heat and where her mother had cooked for a growing family all her married life. Ruth wanted to mention her missing brother, but even the thought of him caused her immediate sadness and she knew that Jonathan's name could only deepen the shadow in her mother's eyes. Hester believed him dead but would not admit her grief at this moment of joy at her elder daughter's return.

It was five o'clock before Becky came in, glowing from a long ride in the keen hill air.

"I'm back!" she announced, throwing her riding hat onto a chair. "It's grand out. We went up over the hill as far as the Butter Tubs and down by Winterside Grange. There wasn't a sign of anyone at the house, although there was a car in the drive. You know it's been sold?" she added to Ruth.

"Mother's been telling me. There seems to be some sort of mystery about the new owner," Ruth added.

"Kate thinks she may be divorced. Anyway, there's no man about the house," Becky said airily. "Only a little boy. He looks about four. I might even be able to sell him Jet," she added with her usual optimism.

"You could wait till you're asked," Hester reminded her. "The widow woman might not want her son to ride."

"I can't imagine why not," Becky returned. "Most children around here can ride by the time they're that age. I was in the saddle before I was four."

"Your father spoiled you," Hester reminded her without rancour. "You were always his blue-eyed bairn."

"Blue-eyed or not," Ruth interrupted, "you can lend a hand in the kitchen, Becky. There are potatoes to peel."

Becky made a face at her. "You're bossing me already!"

"I'm making a useful suggestion," Ruth told her. "After the potatoes you can set the table."

They got on reasonably well together, tolerating each other's whims in spite of the fact that they were so different in character. Outgoing and impulsive in all she did, Becky kept few of her emotions to herself, while Ruth had always thought carefully before making a decision, knowing that it could so easily affect the future. It had taken her a long time to decide to go to London to further her career, but finally she had felt that it was the right thing to do. Becky, on the other hand, had drifted amicably into further education, seeing her years ahead at university as something of an escape from life in the Dales, which she had considered dull.

"There's been a few changes here since you left,"

14

Becky informed her as they worked together. "Not only at the Grange."

She paused, waiting for her sister's reaction.

"You mean High Parks," Ruth said.

"Of course I mean High Parks!" A deep flush stained Becky's cheeks. "It's been bought by some guy who means to breed horses. I've seen him up at the gallops on the high moor and he looks a stunner – all dark-skinned and amazingly handsome, and can he ride!" She let out a deep breath of appreciation. "I plan to meet him one of these days. Soon," she added, "if I have any real luck."

Having thought about her encounter on the moor road more than once since her return home, Ruth confessed, "I think I've already met your Mr Wonderful, and he didn't impress me all that much."

Becky gasped. "You dark horse!" she exclaimed. "You never said!"

"It wasn't important," Ruth declared.

"It is to me," Becky informed her dramatically. "I'm a good rider, but I've grown out of ponies and there isn't a hope of me getting a horse of my own now that money is so tight. I've spoken to one of the stable lads from High Parks and they will be taking on more grooms and even a few riders," she added hopefully.

"They won't want part-timers," Ruth pointed out with an odd sinking feeling in her heart. "You'll be going back to university in October and the new owner will want full-time riders – dedicated people."

"I could be dedicated, given half a chance," Becky declared.

The vehement statement further increased Ruth's unease, but she could not discuss the situation again in her mother's presence.

*　　*　　*

Early the following morning the new owner of High Parks appeared at Lovesome Hill.

Ruth saw him approaching from the sitting-room window and could hardly contain her surprise. She was alone in the house apart from her mother who was still in bed, having been persuaded to stay there for another hour, at least. Becky had gone to Derham on an errand of her own, borrowing Ruth's car because she had been asked to bring back some groceries from Lambert's to last them over the following week.

Her cheeks slightly flushed for no very clear reason, Ruth opened the back door as their unexpected visitor came purposefully across the yard towards the house. He seemed even taller than she had remembered from their first encounter on the moor road and even less approachable, his steely blue eyes encountering hers with slight surprise.

"Yes?" Ruth asked. "Can I help you?"

They had been his own words when they had first met, delivered with an odd reticence in her usually friendly tone, but she supposed he wouldn't even notice that.

"I hope so." He touched his cap, fixing her with a steady gaze. "I had no idea this was where you lived," he added. "I came to see Mrs Kendal."

"I'm Ruth Kendal." She made no effort to hold out her hand in greeting. "My mother won't be able to see you. She has been ill for some time and she's still in bed."

"Hence your return to the dale," he mused. "I'm sorry about your mother's illness. Perhaps I could see her later on?"

Ruth stepped out into the yard, closing the door purposefully behind her. "If you can tell me what you want I may be able to help you," she suggested.

"I heard she might have some land for sale," he

16

offered blandly. "Several acres on the moor, to be exact. I need extended gallops and your land would be ideal."

The 'Useless Pastures', Ruth thought. It was land they seldom used, but it was precious land in a farming community, her brother's birthright. That was how Hester Kendal must look at it. She shook her head.

"I'm afraid not," she said, vainly trying to keep the ice out of her voice. "The Pastures have never been for sale and they never will."

His steady gaze confused her for a moment as he looked back at her in disbelief.

"That's not what I heard," he told her. "Otherwise, I wouldn't be here. I was told your mother would be willing to sell – was even eager to do so."

"You were wrongly informed, in that case." Ruth felt that she had a right to answer for her mother because this man could so easily have taken Hester's consent for granted if he had heard about their circumstances. "We have no land for sale, Mr Bradley, either at Lovesome Hill or the Pastures."

He smiled at her use of his name. "You know who I am," he said. "That isn't too surprising in a community as small as Derham. I thought we might meet again," he added without warmth, "but not like this."

"Perhaps you also thought that an old, sick woman might be a pushover for your desire to obtain more land," Ruth suggested, without quite recognizing the root of her antagonism. "Perhaps you imagined a stranger with money could buy up half the dale without anyone standing in his way."

Sudden anger darkened his eyes for a moment and then he laughed. It was anything but an amused laugh, derisory in its dismissiveness. "I would still like to talk to your mother," he maintained arrogantly. "You see, I believe

17

in going straight to the fountain head when it is a matter of business."

Ruth was quick to recognize his determination, seeing him in that moment as a man who would sweep away everything in his path in order to get what he wanted. "I'm sorry," she said, "but that is quite impossible. I shall be acting for my mother from now on and I think you are wasting your time."

"I hope not," he said, turning away. "The Pastures haven't been fully used since your father died. You run sheep on the hill, but the high land up there is too remote for your present needs. It is ideal for my purpose and for the moment I don't intend to take 'No' for an answer. I'm willing to pay your mother's asking price. Even over the odds. You can tell her that, if you will."

She gasped at what she considered his arrogance. "I don't think you understand what I'm trying to say," she told him. "Money isn't the be-all and end-all of life up here, Mr Bradley. Land is far more important to us. It's our life's blood, something we pass on from one generation to the next, but perhaps you can't understand that since you are a stranger here."

"I'm trying to learn," he answered smoothly, "but I still think I could come to some arrangement with your mother. I've been at High Parks for some time now trying to lick it into shape and I think I'm succeeding where the stables are concerned, but I need more land. That's why I've come cap-in-hand to ask for it," he added with a wry smile, "but I don't seem to be getting anywhere at present."

"You never will!" Ruth said more defiantly than she had intended. "I know my mother and I know the dale. She'll hang onto this land she has cherished all her married life and worked for day after day while she

18

was able. She still thinks of it as her son's inheritance now that my father is dead."

"'Still'?" he queried.

"My brother went abroad before my father died," she told him reluctantly. "We have not heard from him for some time, but that makes no difference. At least, not to my mother. The land is still Jonathan's birthright as far as she is concerned and she won't part with it – to you or anyone else."

"We're not beating about the bush, are we?" His eyes were sharp now, assessing her relentlessly. "You don't intend to give quarter, do you?" His lips twisted in a wry smile. "Well, I can admire that," he admitted, "but I can be equally stubborn in my way. I need this land, Miss Kendal, and I intend to put my argument fair and square to your mother whenever she cares to see me. I'll come again," he promised, "when it is more convenient. Will you tell her that?"

She wanted to tell him that he was wasting his time, that they would never sell their land to anyone under any circumstances, but she was thwarted by her younger sister's immediate arrival. Becky drove her car through the yard gate and across the cobbles, braking to a sudden halt only inches from his Land Rover.

"I know who you are," she told their visitor with all the charm she could muster. "You're our new neighbour at High Parks. My mother will be pleased to see you. I'm Rebecca Kendal," she added for his further enlightenment. "'Becky' for short."

She held out her hand, welcoming the stranger to Lovesome Hill, and Mark Bradley shook it politely, his deeply penetrating gaze on Becky's flushed face. He had gained an accomplice, Ruth thought, exasperated by her sister's eager acceptance of someone they hardly knew.

Was that all? Was Becky's too-easy acceptance of this

man the only thing that worried her or was she just being over-protective of a sister who could very well look after herself? The nagging doubt in her mind about the future made her turn away while Becky watched Mark Bradley climb back into his Land Rover and drive off in the direction of Derham.

"I knew who he was as soon as I saw the Land Rover," Becky declared, following her into the house. "I've seen him driving in and out of the gates at High Parks where he discovered the Stone Birds under the rubble of the old wall. I don't believe in that silly old legend, do you?"

"No – no, I don't." Ruth went on into the warmth of the kitchen. "Can we forget about stone birds and legends and bring in the groceries if you haven't forgotten why you went to Derham in the first place?"

"My! My!" Becky grinned. "We are in a bad mood, aren't we? What had Mark Bradley to say to you that has upset you so much?"

"He wants to buy the Pastures to add them to his existing gallops up there on the moor," Ruth informed her almost reluctantly, "but we will never sell."

"I don't see why not," Becky returned slowly. "We don't use the Pastures very much these days, do we? We've as much land to look after down here as we need around the farm and on the hill. The Pastures would be ideal for him if he wants to extend his gallops and we can't exactly quarrel with that."

"It's not for us to say," Ruth decided sharply. "In the end it can only be Mother's decision."

"You think she wouldn't sell because of Jonathan?" Becky asked. "She won't believe he will never come back to claim his inheritance."

"Neither should we." Ruth's eyes were distressed. "Becky, I wish we really knew what has become of him. He swore he'd never come back while Father was alive, but I think if he knew he was dead he would come now for Mother's sake."

"She'll never really believe he's dead," Becky said quietly, "and we can't distress her by talking about it. Not now."

Becky carried in the groceries, depositing them on the scrubbed surface of the kitchen table.

"If there were some truth in the legend," she remarked casually, "Mark Bradley's luck should be in now that he has restored the Stone Birds to their rightful place. He should have all the luck in the world while they remain there."

Ruth did not answer her, thinking that the new owner of High Parks didn't believe in luck, good or bad, only in his own ability to succeed in everything he did.

In the days that followed she slipped easily enough into an old routine. She had always enjoyed working on the farm and the memories of carefree summer days when the hay was brought in and the sheep were on the high pastures took her back to the carefree pleasures of her youth. Unlike some of the neighbouring dales, Skeldale had a gentle pastoral landscape fairly high up the valley until it finally rose in tiered limestone cliffs to the buttress of the Scar. Some of the lower slopes were shot through with potholes, vertical tunnels bored into the limestone by streams coming off the hillsides, while across the valley the threatening bulk of Whernside dominated the far horizon. Ruth had always thought of the Pennines as the great barrier between her and the rest of the world and now she had come back to settle in the shadow of their comforting security.

This was what she really wanted, she tried to assure herself, this freedom, this chance to shut away the immediate past.

"What happened to you and Tony Grantham?" Becky asked once as they prepared an evening meal in the warm kitchen at Lovesome Hill. "What did you quarrel about?"

Ruth took a full minute to answer her. She had expected the question, knowing that it would come sooner or later, but now that she was face to face with the trauma of unhappy memory she felt at a loss for words. The right words, apparently, to describe a situation she still could hardly understand.

"I suppose we – just drifted apart," she answered slowly at last. "Tony wanted what he called 'space' to think about the future and I suppose I needed reassurance. I wanted to know where the years ahead were going for both of us, what they would hold or not hold." She drew a quick breath. "Tony's freedom meant a great deal to him," she added, "and he wasn't prepared to give it up."

Becky looked at her speculatively. "You're better without him," she said less sensitively than she need have done. "I never liked him."

"You only met him twice," Ruth reminded her with the ghost of a smile. "Once in London and once when I brought him up here to meet Mother. Hardly time for you to judge."

"Maybe not." Becky turned from the table. "But I've got a feeling about these things. Call it 'fey' if you like, but I'm generally right."

Ruth nodded indulgently. "While we're on the delicate subject of romance and the future," she asked, "how do you feel about Charles Oliver? It would be more than handy to have a vet in the family."

"Oh – Chay!" Becky made a face. "He's all right, but he's far too stuffy. He can only think of animals and building up his practice. Besides, he's far too old."

"Not a day over thirty, I'd guess," Ruth declared. "You could do a lot worse than Chay."

"I'm not interested." Becky tossed her head. "Of course, I'm fond of Chay, but not in that way. He's clever with cattle and dogs and horses, but he's so – stolid. He even dresses like a farmer."

"Does that mean you've met someone special in York?" Ruth asked, aware of a sudden tell-tale flush on her sister's glossy cheeks.

"Nobody in particular," Becky said. "You meet lots and lots of men in college, but it doesn't mean you want to marry them. I prefer sophisticated men."

"Do you now?" Ruth laughed. "Like anyone I know?"

The flush on Becky's cheeks deepened. "No," she declared, "and I'm not telling. He doesn't live too far away."

"And with that we must be satisfied." Ruth turned from the Aga. "Have fun while you can," she said.

The following morning Mark Bradley came back to Lovesome Hill. He was no longer driving his high-powered Land Rover but rode a handsome grey mare instead. Clad in riding breeches and a well-cut hacking jacket he looked born to the saddle and Becky drew in a swift appreciative breath as she went forward to meet him.

Ruth had called off the dogs. Silver and her son, Wraith, bounded out of the barn to greet every stranger with loud barking, settling down only when they considered that the visitor was accepted by the family at large. She had no idea why the new owner of High Parks should have sought them out again after their last encounter and she left Becky to do the talking.

"Would you like to come in," her sister invited. "We were just going to have some coffee. You'd be welcome."

Mark Bradley turned to Ruth with the faintest of smiles.

"If you're sure of that," he said to the welcoming Becky. "As a matter of fact, I came to see your mother."

Going straight to the fountain head, Ruth thought, flushing in her turn, though not with pleasure. She watched their unexpected visitor dismount. In the immaculately tailored breeches which hugged his thighs above the polished length of his boots, his body tapering to a narrow waist, he looked taller than ever, his broad shoulders accentuated by the expert cut of his jacket. Easily he dropped from the saddle, stepping aside to allow Ruth to enter the house before him.

"I didn't expect to see you again," she told him.

"You didn't think I'd have the effrontry to come back, I suppose you mean." His dominating eyes challenged hers with the faintest amusement in their depths, steel-blue eyes she had not been able to forget.

The two collies followed them in and she lingered in the warmth of the kitchen to settle them, aware of her reluctance to escort Mark Bradley into the family sitting-room where her mother was reading the local paper. Of course he had come to renew his request for the land they owned, but the Pastures were still not for sale. His persuasive powers would be useless and he would go away with a flea in his ear.

"I'll make the coffee," she offered to Becky's satisfaction. "Mother, you have a visitor," she added reluctantly.

She saw Hester struggle from her chair and Mark Bradley settling her back into it before she closed the sitting-room door. Becky made no effort to follow her.

What did Mark Bradley really want? The coveted Pastures, of course, but it could hardly be their friendship. He was obviously a law unto himself, with little or no inhibitions to deter him when he was bent on getting his own way, but he would come up against the Dales' stubborn pride and he wouldn't always win. She was quite sure of that.

Making the coffee, she stood with her back to the door leading into the hall, waiting for it to percolate. Becky shouldn't be encouraging him. They must leave any final decision to their mother and she knew what that would be, she concluded. Her brow creased in a frown, she stared down at the Aga. It was amazing effrontry for him to have come at all.

"Can I help?"

She swung round to confront him standing in the doorway with that faintly amused smile on his lips.

"I can manage," she declared stiffly. "I'll follow you back through – if you mean to stay."

His smile deepened, although there was a sudden hardness to the cast of his square jaw which warned against argument.

"I've accepted your mother's hospitality," he reminded her. "She's an easy person to talk to."

"But not so easy to impress." She set the coffee-pot firmly on the tray she had prepared with four cups and saucers and a plate of home-made biscuits. "If you've come about the land you're still wasting your time. Sugar?"

"Please." He took up the tray. "I have come about the Pastures, but I also thought I should be neighbourly and pay a social call now that I have finally settled in."

"It's taken you some time, I gather," she remarked acidly. "Becky says you've been here for six months."

"Ah – Becky!" he said. "She has certainly been kind."

Angry at letting him see that he had been discussed so intimately, Ruth led the way across the hall back into the sitting-room where Becky had pulled an occasional table over to her mother's chair. Mark Bradley set the heavy tray down at Hester's side while Ruth bent to replenish the fire from the pile of logs on the open hearth.

"Sit yourself down," Hester invited. "I always find a man standing around fills the place up. What have you done at High Parks that we don't already know about?"

"I haven't done much to the house. I'm leaving that till later since it doesn't matter so much." Mark sat down on the saddle-chair at her elbow, looking amazingly at home, and it was plain that Hester already liked him. "I've been buying livestock. Mostly horses."

"We heard," Becky said. "How many horses?"

Ruth passed him the sugar.

"Four at present. The others will follow in a day or two."

"You'll need lots of help," Becky observed. "Extra help," she added deliberately.

Ruth felt the colour rising in her cheeks. In a moment her irresponsible sister was going to ask him for a job. A summer job, at least.

"I ride very well," Becky informed him unashamedly.

Mark smiled at her. "I'll keep that in mind," he promised, "but I've just hired another groom."

"Becky wouldn't be any good to you," Hester informed him with her usual blunt candour. "She'll be going back to university in October. She's at York."

"I need a holiday job," Becky protested. "It would fill in the time. You could get bored just doing housework all day."

"There's plenty to do about the farm," Hester pointed out. "If you want to ride you can always borrow a horse. You did yesterday."

"Suppose so!" Becky was hardly convinced. "I can't depend on getting a mount from Kate every day, especially if her brother is coming home," she pointed out sulkily.

"I hadn't heard that," Hester said, her dark eyes suddenly wistful. "Kate and Ruth are childhood friends and they and – my son went to school together," she explained to their visitor, pausing a moment to look deep into the happier past. "The Metcalfs' farm is over on the far side of Derham above the Lynchets," she added. "You get to it by the back road across the packhorse bridge if you're interested."

"I'll remember," Mark assured her, although he did not promise to visit the Metcalf farm even at a later date.

Because they had no land to sell, Ruth thought cynically. Nothing that he really wanted.

He came to the thorny subject of the Pastures as she lifted the tray to carry it back into the kitchen.

"Mrs Kendal," he said, "I need some more land."

Ruth set the tray back onto the table between him and her mother.

"What kind of land?" Hester asked, interested in something she really knew about.

"Good land that's not being used to its full potential at present," he said.

"You mean our Pastures?" Hester looked him straight in the eye. "What would you be meaning to do with it if I did agree to sell?"

Ruth held her breath.

"I need longer gallops." Mark settled himself back into the saddle-chair. "The land I own up there isn't long enough," he explained. "It's right for my purpose at present, but it won't be when I expand. I need longer runs and the Pastures are adjacent to my property. I understand you haven't used them for some time and I wondered if you would be willing to sell."

He hadn't looked at Ruth, but she felt that he was aware of her reaction, of the instant tightening of her lips and the hostility in her eyes. Her mother could see it, she supposed, sitting there facing her, but Hester was making her own decision.

"I've never given it a thought," she said, meeting the proposition head on. "It's always been good land, but we've cut down our flock since my husband died and for other reasons," she added. "Help is hard to come by up here, as you may already have noticed and I'm handicapped now to a certain extent, but I'm not thinking of selling any of our land."

Ruth took up the tray with a little smile of satisfaction playing about her lips. She could leave matters in her mother's hands now as indeed she must.

Mark Bradley opened the sitting-room door for her.

"I can manage," she said, although he had not offered to help her with the tray.

Becky stayed behind in the sitting-room, not offering to help either. Ruth could hear their voices through the open kitchen door as a faint murmur, her mother's quietly assured, Mark Bradley's devoid of argument now that he had come face to face with the truth. No way would a proud and purposeful woman like Hester Kendal sell land that was once her son's inheritance even now that she might reluctantly believe him dead.

Occasionally Becky's high-pitched laughter broke through, but Ruth supposed this was just her sister's way of impressing Mark with her own impartiality.

When their unexpected visitor did decide to leave she was still in the kitchen preparing their midday meal. He stood behind her for a moment, waiting for her to turn from the sink, and she could feel his eyes on her rigid back assessing her relentlessly.

"You may think I've won," Ruth heard herself saying in some sort of defence, "but the final decision was always with my mother. I only told you what to expect."

"In no uncertain manner." His voice was low and still

slightly amused for a man who had come up against defeat. "I admire your mother," he said. "She doesn't beat about the bush. She calls a spade a spade. That's what I like. It saves time and a lot of anguish."

She turned to face him. "I'm sorry if you've been disappointed," she said.

He came close, standing head and shoulders above her in the bright sunshine streaming in through the window. "No, you're not," he said firmly. "You're highly elated and you want to say 'I told you so!' That's a fact, isn't it?"

"I don't believe in stating the obvious," Ruth defended herself, "but you evidently know nothing about the Yorkshire Dales."

"About your stubborn determination to hold out for a principle?" he queried, dark eyebrows raised. "Oh, yes, I do. I wasn't brought up all that far away. On the other side of the Pennines in fact, and I understand about property – especially land. I didn't expect your mother to sell out to me without question, as a matter of fact."

"Then – what made you try so hard?" Ruth demanded.

"Against your excellent advice?" His eyebrows were still raised in an amused arch. "Maybe I don't take advice very easily."

For a moment it looked as if he wanted to shake her and indeed he could have done since they were so close together, and then he smiled.

"Your mother and I have struck a bargain," he said. "It was one I hadn't thought about, but it suits my purpose very well. We have agreed a lease on the Pastures for three years. After that we may come to a final decision."

Ruth let out her breath in a long sigh.

"Disappointed?" he asked.

She smoothed the hair back from her forehead. "Why should I be?" she demanded. "It's not my land."

"But you felt strongly about it? I don't blame you," he acknowledged, "so perhaps we can let sleeping dogs lie?" He held out his hand to her. "At least we might be friends."

Ruth could not snub him again, not now that the question of the Pastures had been amicably settled, and she felt her hand encompassed in a hard grip as his fingers tightened over her own.

"We'll meet, of course," he said. "It's hardly impossible in a place so small and remote as Derham."

"I hardly think so," Ruth said, wondering why she should still feel animosity towards this man. "We will both be leading busy lives from now on and High Parks and Lovesome Hill are really miles apart. I have to make this farm pay, Mr Bradley. It isn't just something that is here for my amusement."

"Like High Parks," he suggested with a brief smile. "But you are so wrong. I'm not pumping surplus money into a stud simply to amuse myself. This venture has to pay its way, too." He took a stride towards the outer door. "You see, it's something of a challenge as far as I'm concerned," he added. "I've always been assured of inheriting the family business and all that goes with it, but in some ways that hasn't been enough. As you can imagine, I'm arrogant enough to want to succeed on my own account. You can hardly blame me for that."

"I can't think that my opinion matters," Ruth told him.

An eyebrow shot up. "You could be right," he said. "I make my own decisions in the end."

She held open the door for him.

"Will you cut the Pastures off from local use?" she asked curiously. "Fence it in, perhaps?"

He shook his head. "Not at present," he decided. "If the locals went to go up there they're welcome so long as they don't interfere with the gallops."

30

"They're not likely to do that," Ruth protested. "They're country people used to animals. They'll respect your need to train your horses in a convenient place."

He turned to look at her as he went out. "You don't agree with your mother's decision, do you?" he asked. "You would rather someone local made such a bargain with her." His eyes narrowed a little. "For all your recent sojourn in the big, sophisticated world south of the Pennines you're still a Daleswoman at heart, pig-headed about selling land to a stranger. When it comes down to brass tacks you would never give in. You would never meet anyone half-way as your mother has done because you are determined and stubborn in your beliefs."

Ruth's eyes glittered as they met his. "Believe what you will," she challenged. "The point is that you don't know me at all and you're not very sure about the people who have lived here all their lives. You have a lot to learn, Mr Bradley, and I hope it won't be too difficult for you to take 'No' for an answer the next time you decide to impose your will on the community at large."

Exasperatingly, he looked amused. "So far, so good," he smiled, pulling his riding-hat down over his brow. "At least I flatter myself that I have made a friend of your mother – and Becky," he added.

Becky came rushing through from the sitting-room to see him off, standing beside the grey mare as he untethered her from the hitching post.

"You said you had a pony for sale," Ruth heard him say. "I could be interested."

She watched them walk together towards the gate, talking companionably, but he did not return to inspect the pony, although she was sure her sister had supplied him with all the details if she thought that he was even remotely interested in a sale. Becky remained at the gate watching as he rode away.

31

"Guess what?" she demanded when she found Ruth still at the kitchen sink.

"I couldn't in a thousand years," Ruth said, "so tell me."

"He wants to buy Jet."

"Oh? Well, you did say poor old Jet was no use to you."

"He's offered me a terrific price for him."

"And you've agreed to sell. Just like that?"

"You know I'll be heartbroken to part with Jet." Becky drew a hand across her eyes. "I love that pony."

"Where is Mark Bradley going to keep him?" Ruth asked. "At High Parks?"

Becky shook her head. "He's buying Jet for a friend."

"A very small friend, surely?"

"Well – a friend's little boy. He'll be at Winterside Grange," Becky explained. "Not too far away if I want to see him occasionally."

Ruth turned to look at her. "That must be the widow's child," she suggested. "He's certainly getting friendly with the neighbours."

"So he should." Becky sampled a jam puff Ruth had taken from the oven earlier. "Even you said that."

"I wonder how he got to know the people at the Grange," Ruth mused.

"Maybe they got together because they were both strangers in the dale. It could happen," Becky decided. "Anyway, he's coming back to take a look at Jet in a day or two, so don't go putting him off."

"As if I would!" Ruth took a fruit pie from the oven to lay it on a cooling rack. "I hope he won't disappoint you. What are you going to do with the money?"

"Give it to Mother, of course," Becky said. "What did you think?"

"I haven't the vaguest idea. How did Mark Bradley know you wanted to sell Jet?" Ruth asked.

"I mentioned it while you were out of the room and he was discussing the Pastures with Mother," Becky told her. "He seemed interested right away."

"I see."

"No you don't! You're utterly prejudiced where Mark Bradley is concerned," Becky accused her. "Why do you think that is?"

"He struck me as being far too masterful even when we first met," Ruth confessed. "Far too sure of himself and all he wanted from life."

"That's no mean thing," her sister countered. "If you're not sure what you want from life you'll never get anywhere. I'm glad old Jet isn't going very far," she added, "and I'll be able to see him whenever I like."

"Don't count your chickens!" Ruth warned. "You haven't met the new owner of the Grange yet."

"Neither have you," Becky retorted, sampling another jam puff. "She can't be very old when her son is under five. Five next birthday, Mark said." She paused on her way out to the yard where the two collies were waiting for her expectantly. "He's quite something," she decided reminiscently. "Mark Bradley will change this dale. Take my word for it. He's that sort of person. You won't be able to fight him, Ruth, so why try? He would always win."

Her words echoed hollowly against the silence as the quiet house recovered from the impact of her buoyant personality. Becky had always been the outgoing one, ever ready for adventure of any sort, and her presence must have been missed at Lovesome Hill by her mother, at least. She was more like George Kendal than Ruth and she was certainly the daughter he had loved most.

Going through to the sitting-room Ruth found her mother in a thoughtful mood.

33

"Has Becky told you what we have arranged?" Hester asked. "I know I should have consulted you first, but it wasn't like selling out altogether. Mark Bradley was most persuasive, but I think he's an honest man and the extra money will help towards Becky's future. I was finding it a bit of a strain, to tell you the truth," she confessed, "though I would never have let her know. She must have her chance and I think you agree."

Ruth sat down beside her. "Of course I agree," she said, "and I hope she appreciates what you are doing for her."

"Her father would have done it whatever the cost," Hester reminded her. "He was a hard man in many ways, but he wasn't lacking in ambition for his family. He was proud of you, too, Ruth – of all you had achieved."

"I can accept that," Ruth agreed. "I only wish he had made it a bit more obvious."

"You were always the dependable one," Hester assured her. "I could always feel you were there when I needed you. As for Becky," she added slowly, "I can't be sure. She's strong-willed and impetuous and she lets her enthusiasms run away with her. For a while I thought she was happy enough with Chay Oliver – him being the local vet and interested in the same things – but since she has gone to York she seems to have changed her mind. I know Chay is over ten years older than she is, but that isn't a bad thing with someone as volatile as Becky."

"The steadying influence, you mean," Ruth smiled. "Becky's hardly in the mood to be steadied at present, although I think she is fond enough of Chay. Growing up with someone isn't exactly what Becky wants at present."

Hester sighed. "I suppose not," she agreed. "We'll just have to hope for the best while we wait and see."

To Ruth's horror Becky didn't leave them long in

34

suspense about the future. The very next day while they were walking the dogs along the summer meadow she brought up the subject of York.

"I'm not going back to university," she announced decisively. "I've changed my mind."

Ruth halted in her tracks, shocked by the sheer unexpectedness of her sister's decision. "What do you mean 'you're not going back'?" she asked. "You're enrolled for a three-year course. You can't just opt out at a moment's notice on a sudden whim."

"It isn't sudden," Becky objected. "I've thought about it for months. I'm not cut out for an academic life, sitting and passing exams and all that sort of thing, never feeling free."

"Free to do what?" Ruth felt as if a trickle of ice-cold water had run down her spine. "Can you explain it to me, for I just can't imagine why you're throwing away such a wonderful chance?"

"I expected you to react like this," Becky accused her. "You've never had this thing about the dale, about riding free across the moor and being your own mistress when it comes to breeding horses. You think that's a man's job, don't you? You can see Mark Bradley doing it, but not your puny little sister. Well—" She drew a deep breath. "I can tell you even if I have to start from the very bottom I'm still going to work with horses, so you needn't bother trying to talk me out of it."

"I thought I would be trying to make you see sense," Ruth countered. "Have you thought about what this is going to mean to Mother, especially at the moment?"

Becky's bright face clouded over. "That's the worst part," she acknowledged. "I don't know how to tell her."

"And you would like me to?" Ruth's shock had turned to anger now. "I won't do it, Becky. I won't inflict that sort of hurt on her, even for you."

35

They walked in silence for a moment through the knee-high grass which had always been a delight to them at this season of the year when the meadow was studded with wild flowers – buttercups and meadow-sweet and daisies and tiny purple orchids nestling close to the ground to make a fragrant carpet at their feet. The dogs loved it, bounding joyously ahead of them to disappear over the hill towards the high road. Before the hay was mown it had always been Ruth's favourite place, but now it was suddenly, ruthlessly changed. Becky's determination hung over it like a cloud, a cloud so dark that she could hardly see the sun.

"Will you let me offer you some advice?" she asked, at last.

"Advise away!" Becky agreed.

"Give all this a little more thought," Ruth pleaded. "You've got all the long summer vacation to change your mind. Breeding horses doesn't come easily – or cheaply, and you haven't got that sort of money to spend."

"I can start at the bottom," Becky declared. "I'm prepared to do that."

"Even so," Ruth pointed out, "it is something you have to be sure about."

"I am sure – absolutely sure. I've always worked with animals and that's what I want to do. I've got a way with them. Surely you're going to agree about that? I could ride a pony before I was five. Father taught me and it sort of gets into your blood. Can't you understand that?" Becky demanded.

"In a way." Ruth was thinking ahead, desperate to shield her mother from further hurt. "Couldn't you give York another year, Becky – give yourself time to think again and maybe to change your mind? You're still only eighteen. You have all your life before you."

"Sometimes you talk like a very old woman!" Becky

retorted. "Were you always so sensible when you were my age?"

"I made mistakes," Ruth was quick to admit. "I didn't always listen to sweet reason even when I was older than you are now, but that's not the point, is it? All I'm asking you to do is to give yourself time and not throw away a terrific opportunity in a moment of enthusiasm for something else."

"How much time?" Becky wanted to know.

"Till you can see everything more clearly," Ruth said. "At the present moment you haven't even got a horse of your own to ride."

"That's true," Becky agreed, thinking ahead.

Chapter Two

When they reached Lovesome Hill a familiar figure was leaning against the paddock gate talking to Jet. The shaggy little pony had come up to greet their visitor, eyes alert, head down, waiting to be scratched behind the ears. Both sheep-dogs had run ahead of them and were lying crouched on the grass verge of the road waiting for his first words of command.

"Hullo, Amos!" Ruth greeted the old shepherd in some surprise. "How are you?"

Amos Farley straightened himself with an effort, turning to greet her with a toothless smile. "No better than I should be, Miss Ruth," he declared, leaning on the heavy walking-stick he carried. "I thought I'd take a turn round the fields to see if there was owt I could do for thee, but nowt seems to be spoilin' wi' you in charge."

"I don't know about that, Amos," Ruth smiled. "I'm only an amateur, after all. I've got a lot to learn."

"Farming's bred in thee," he told her, turning to look at Becky for the first time. "I'd have a word with veterinary about this animal o' yours," he advised. "He won't be much use if you're meanin' to part wi' him when he's walkin' lame."

"I hadn't noticed." Becky was beside him in an instant, full of concern as she fondled Jet's shaggy head. "What's the matter with you, old thing?" she asked gently. "You can't go lame on me now, of all things. I've found you

38

a new home and you'll be very happy. It isn't too far away," she consoled as the pony gazed back at her with sombre eyes.

Ruth turned sharply away.

"I'll phone the surgery," she offered. "Amos, are you coming up to the house for a drink of tea?"

She led the way towards the back door with the old shepherd hobbling after her while Becky slipped through the paddock gate to examine the pony's injury. Jet's eager whinney of delight sped across the paddock in their wake.

"Happen you need some help," Amos suggested when Ruth had phoned the surgery in Derham and left her message. "Happen you've bitten off more than you can chew."

"I hope not, Amos," Ruth said, aware that his eagle eye had detected some of the disarray in the barns. "I thought I was managing fine."

"You haven't come to the shearing yet," he pointed out reasonably enough. "That'll test thee. Happen I could spare thee a day or two."

She smiled at his diplomacy. "Give yourself time, Amos," she cautioned. "When you're really fit to come back to work we'll be glad to have you."

He sat himself down beside the Aga while she made the tea and presently her mother hobbled through from the sitting-room to see who she was talking to.

"It's you, Amos," Hester observed in some surprise. "How did you get here?"

"On my own two feet, Missus," the old shepherd informed her importantly. "I've walked all my life, as tha' knows, an' I canna abide sittin' idle all day. I'm gettin' by fine enough wi' a stick, like thi'sen."

Hester laughed. "We must beat each other to it, Amos," she said, turning to Ruth. "I thought I heard you on the phone."

"You did. I was trying to get through to Chay, but I could only get his answer-phone. Amos thinks Jet is walking lame and we'd better see what Chay can do about it."

"You can rely on Chay," Hester said. "He'll be up at one of the farms, but I guess he'll be here within the hour. He's got one of those fancy new phones you can carry around with you so they'll let him know as soon as somebody clears the answer-phone at the surgery."

She had always been fond of the local veterinary surgeon, mothering him at times when she felt he needed it, and Charles Oliver had been more than grateful. He had no family of his own and he knew that Hester's interest in him was completely genuine. The thought never crossed his mind that it had a lot to do with Becky, although he made no secret of his infatuation with her younger daughter. If Becky sometimes treated him disgracefully he was prepared to live with that, quite sure that she would eventually change.

In under an hour he drove his battered old Vauxhall up to the farmhouse door, going direct to the paddock where Becky was waiting for him. Ruth watched their two fair heads bent over the pony, thinking how alike they were in looks, at least. They were both fair-haired and fair-skinned with the ruddy look of the outdoors about them, as if they had lived all their lives in the face of the wind up here on the moor. They were both sturdy and slightly below average height and they were both crazy about animals. So much in common, Ruth mused, yet Becky had other thoughts about love.

Chay Oliver took his bag from the Vauxhall to begin his work while Becky held Jet's head steady, obviously soothing him with her words of comfort. In half an hour it was all over and they were walking towards the back door.

"It was nothing much," Becky said. "Just some hard skin growing over a bit of flint he had picked up in his hoof a while ago. I hadn't noticed him limping till Amos pointed it out."

Amos made for the door. "I'll be on my way," he said. "Think on about help when tha' comes to need it."

"Thanks, Amos," Becky said, genuinely grateful.

"Can I give you a lift as far as The Byres?" Chay asked. "I'm going that way."

"If tha' must," Amos agreed. "I could walk just the same."

"No need to walk when I've got four wheels under me," Chay told him cheerfully. "I was thinking of dropping in to see you, anyway." He looked across the kitchen to where Becky was standing. "Will you be going to the barbecue?" he asked. "Over at the Metcalfs'."

"Sure," Becky said. "I've already been invited. I thought you might have been too busy."

"'All work and no play'," Chay quoted. "Can I pick you up? I'll be passing your road-end."

"If you like," Becky said without much enthusiasm.

"There will be plenty of people there," Chay encouraged her. "Kate's making it a bit of a party for the people at the Grange. She believes we ought to fraternize."

"So she says," Becky answered. "I wonder if that means Mark Bradley will be going."

"Bradley? Oh, yes, the new chap at High Parks," Chay remembered. "I haven't met him yet, but it's said he's something of a loner. Only comes to Derham on business and he probably has his own vet. Certainly he hasn't contacted me so far."

"He'll get round to it," Becky said. "And you're busy enough as it is."

"That's true." Chay turned to pay his respects to Hester who encouraged him to "come again any time".

41

"I will," he said, "so long as you don't get tired of having me."

Becky walked as far as the paddock with him to take another look at Jet.

"I wish she wouldn't be so abrupt with him," Hester sighed. "She could do a lot worse than settle down with Chay Oliver."

Thinking about her disturbing conversation with her sister in the summer meadow Ruth said guardedly, "She's not in the settling mood yet. Becky has a whole lot of thinking to do before she'll even consider marriage to Chay or anybody else."

For some reason her thoughts had flown to Mark Bradley, although she had no reason to believe that Becky would ever become involved with the new owner of High Parks even by the remotest chance.

The young veterinary surgeon had done his work well and Jet was soon galloping round the paddock, eager to be out on the moor to fill his lungs with the keen hill air. So far there had been no further word from Mark Bradley about the sale although he had phoned Hester on two occasions about the lease of the Pastures which he was having drawn up officially by a solicitor in Derham.

"He's changed his mind about Jet," Becky said, disappointed. "I wish he hadn't seemed so keen in the first place."

"Give him time," Hester advised. "He sounds like a busy man to me."

Too busy to remember his promise to a little boy? Ruth could not believe he would be so insensitive, but, then, she hardly knew him. If he had made the promise to the child to impress his mother he would surely keep it, she reasoned, not without a twinge of something like envy in her heart.

Shaking herself mentally, she turned back to work.

Unlike Becky, she was never likely to meet 'the widow woman' who had taken up residence among them and who seemed to be as much of a recluse as Mark himself.

With hay-making and the shearing rapidly approaching, she had little time to spare. There was a barn to be cleared out and a floor to scrub before they could lay the sheared fleece cleanly on the boards as they had always done and Becky wasn't exactly willing to help. She generally found some sort of excuse to be elsewhere and the first wet morning in over a week was no exception.

"I'll go for the butcher-meat," she offered, "if I can borrow your car."

"Don't be too long," Ruth called after her when she had handed over the car keys. "I'm starting on the barn."

"Must we?" Becky asked.

"It's an ideal day for it," Ruth said. "Misty and damp. We'll not be interrupted."

"Rather you than me!" Becky declared as she drove away.

When she had settled her mother before the sitting-room fire Ruth donned a pair of workman-like jeans, thrusting her feet into a pair of wellingtons to keep them free from the mud. The thick sweater she wore came down to her knees and she tied a scarf over her hair to keep it free from dust.

Thus equipped, she set to work, moving bales of straw and crates and farm implements into the smaller barn before she began her final task of scrubbing the boards. It was like old times, she mused, except that she had never worked alone before. There had always been Amos and her father and Jonathan in the beginning.

Thinking of her absent brother, her eyes misted over with tears, wishing him back at Lovesome Hill where he belonged. Was he dead? Had he really gone forever? She

43

could not believe it as she applied herself to her task with renewed vigour, kneeling on the rubber mat to scrub the first board.

"Hullo!" a voice said behind her. "Can I come in?"

She turned her head, sitting back on her heels to confront her visitor. All she could see at first was a pair of highly polished riding boots and then her eyes travelled upwards to the immaculate jodhpurs and beautifully tailored jacket and silk shirt which completed the stranger's outfit.

"I'm Emma Falconer," her visitor informed her. "I've come over from Winterside Grange to look at your pony."

Ruth struggled to her feet, acutely aware of her unkempt appearance in the face of the other woman's beauty. Emma Falconer was the loveliest creature she had seen for many a year. Her brilliant dark eyes, wide and luminous, were fringed by long black eyelashes which owed nothing to artifice and her skin was like pale marble framed by luxuriant black hair which she wore in a tidy chignon at the back of her shapely head. The only splash of colour was her full red lips, parted now in a friendly smile.

Conscious of the rough sacking apron she had tied round her waist, Ruth wiped her hands on it before she shook her visitor's proffered hand. Long cool fingers closed over hers as they looked into each other's eyes. What colour were Emma's eyes? she wondered. Blue as dark midnight, grey like slate, perhaps, or deepest violet? It was hard to tell.

"I'm afraid I'm not Jet's owner," she found herself apologizing. "My sister has gone to Derham to do some shopping and I'm not sure when she's due back."

"I think I saw Jet down in the field beside the gate as I rode past," Emma said. "He looked a dear and Mark thinks

44

he's just what we want for Harry. I never question Mark's judgement where horses are concerned," she smiled. "He has been so good to us, finding Winterside for me at short notice and taking an awful lot of responsibility off my shoulders. Do you think I might wait till your sister comes home?" She looked back at the gelding she had tethered to the hitching-post at the far side of the yard. "If I'd be holding you up please go on with what you were doing," she added. "I can walk down and talk to Jet."

Hastily Ruth untied the offending piece of sacking from around her waist.

"Will you come up to the house?" she asked. "My sister won't be long and I was just about to make some tea."

"If you're sure? Emma hesitated. "You looked so busy down there on your knees scrubbing away. I had no idea barns had to be spring-cleaned."

"We do it before we start to shear the sheep in a few weeks' time. It makes for cleaner wool," Ruth explained, "so it's well worth the effort in the end."

"It looks like hard work, all the same," Emma observed. "Have you always worked on the farm, Miss Kendal?"

"For much of my life," Ruth agreed, "but I did spend several years in London till a month ago as PA to the managing director of an advertising company."

"Indeed?" Emma looked surprised. "What brought you back to Derham?"

"Necessity, I expect." Ruth was determined not to look too deeply into the past. "My mother is only just recovering from a stroke and I felt I was needed."

"Mark calls you a 'House of Women' – in the best meaning of the words, of course. He explained that your father is dead," Emma said.

"Yes. I suppose that's why I really came back. My mother needed me because she had no one else to depend on. I don't regret my choice," Ruth added truthfully. "I'm not missing London one little bit."

"I'd be surprised if you did. I've lived there most of my life," Emma said, "and all the time I was married." Her eyes saddened. "I'm glad I took Mark's advice and came away."

They had reached the house where Hester had been watching their progress from the sitting-room window. Proudly Ruth ushered their visitor in by the back door.

"We don't use the front very much," she explained. "It's where all the wind is. It has to be a special occasion." Immediately she was sorry for the remark which might have been mistaken for a snub. "It's a way we have in the Dales," she added briefly. "Come through and meet my mother."

She discarded her dusty headgear in the hall as Emma Falconer followed her almost eagerly.

"I'm still in a bit of a turmoil at the Grange," she confessed. "It's such a large place to put straight and I've got furniture to buy. Mark says I should be able to pick up an antique or two locally, but I want to take my time. I don't want to make mistakes."

"There's an auction mart over at Layburn in Wensley-dale," Ruth offered, "and there's plenty of small places, too. You can't go wrong."

"Mark's not into that sort of thing," Emma smiled. "It's horses or nothing as far as he's concerned."

They were surely very close, Ruth thought, this woman and the man who had practically shut himself away at High Parks, and she could quite understand if he found Emma Falconer attractive. What man wouldn't?

"Mother," she announced at the sitting-room door, "you've got a visitor."

Hester was standing beside her favourite armchair when Emma Falconer walked in. She had a reasonably good idea who her visitor might be because all her near neighbours were familiar to her and Emma was not quite like any of them. Her appearance spoke sophistication for one thing and she had apparently not ridden very far because she looked fresh and relaxed. There was also a sort of diffidence about her which suggested shyness, although her smile was warm.

"I hope I'm not disturbing you," she said, shaking Hester's proffered hand. "I came over to see your daughter's pony. Mark recommended it because he thought it would be just right for Harry – my small son who is only four."

"As right as it could be," Hester agreed, making room for her beside the fire. "Sit yourself down and have some tea. Becky will be back soon and show you round. She's outgrown Jet who's been eating his head off since she's been away at the university in York."

"Maybe your daughter won't want to sell Jet?" Emma suggested sympathetically.

"A girl never wants to part with her first pony," Hester informed her, "and Becky's small for her age. It's different for a boy. He changes his horses willingly enough, believing himself a grown man before his time. I see you've ridden over from Winterside," she observed. "Are you well settled at the Grange?"

"I'm here to stay," Emma told her, "but I wouldn't say I was completely settled in. There has been so much to do – moving up from London, saying goodbyes and – and that sort of thing."

"You'll miss your friends," Hester supposed, "but you've plenty of room at Winterside to entertain them when they come."

Emma's face clouded over for a moment before she said, "I hope to make other friends here, especially for Harry's sake. That's why I would like him to get out and

47

about in the dale as much as possible while the weather is good."

"Has he been ill?" Hester asked bluntly.

Emma hesitated. "Not really. He has always been rather weakly since he was born. That is why I have been persuaded to bring him away from London."

"You couldn't have found him a better place," Hester assured her as Ruth brought in the tea-tray. "The dale will put colour into his cheeks in no time and give him backbone. Within a year you'll hardly know him."

"I hope you're right," Emma smiled. "It's exactly what Mark thinks, although I tell him he's absurdly biased in that respect."

"Biased, nothing!" Hester declared. "The north country air is second to none. It's even put back the roses into Ruth's cheeks already and you've only to look at her to see she's content."

Emma did look at Ruth, but it was more out of curiosity than agreement with her hostess. What she saw was a daughter who was very like her mother in so many ways, although several years in London had blunted her native candour to a certain extent. She saw a young woman in her early twenties who would speak her mind, yet she was conscious of a reserve in Ruth which was difficult to explain. She knew that she had tangled with Mark in the beginning over his request to buy some land, but apart from that she had hoped that they would become friends.

"People are being kind," she told Hester as Ruth poured the tea. "I've been invited to a party at Derham by some people called Metcalf who have a daughter called Kate."

Ruth smiled. "We know the Metcalfs very well," she agreed. "Kate and I went to school together in Derham. We've lived here all our lives."

48

"Until you went to London," Emma mused. "You must have missed Kate."

"Very much," Ruth said. "Kate's the sort of person one can rely on." She handed over Emma's cup. "She's very much like a sister as far as I am concerned because we are the same age. She has a younger brother and all the family work very hard on the farm and in the business in the town. They give a party every year. You are sure to enjoy it."

Emma's smile was enigmatic. "I've never been to a barbecue," she confessed almost sheepishly. "It sounds like fun and Mark thinks I ought to go."

She seemed to rely a great deal on Mark's opinion, Ruth thought, yet she was not without decisiveness on her own account.

"I'll give it a try," she said. "Once Harry has gone to bed there's very little for me to do at the Grange except work."

"You're too young to be shutting yourself up in a big house on your own," Hester observed bluntly. "You'll be better for the company once you get out and about."

Emma's answering smile was almost wistful. "So I'm told," she agreed. "I must make the effort now that I am here."

"Don't let anyone tell you that it takes thirty years to be accepted in the Dales," Hester advised. "It all depends on yourself and how you respond. We're not folks to make a great fuss of you but we'll help you all we can to settle yourself in. You and the boy," she added kindly.

"Thank you," Emma said, turning her head away.

Over the teacups they discussed London up to a point, and the weather and how lovely the dale looked in full summer and even in the winter weather when it snowed.

"Harry will love it," Ruth decided, "and there are plenty of children around in Denham to befriend him."

Hester and Emma seemed to get on immediately. Hester's blunt, unequivocal approach delighted their unexpected visitor and before she left Emma was promising to call again.

"Can we pick up Jet and call again at the weekend?" she asked before they parted. "Mark has a horse-box he can let me have and I'd like to meet your sister."

"She should have been back from Derham by now," Ruth said, "but you never can tell with Becky. She always meets someone she knows and goes off at a tangent regardless of time. Will you bring your little boy with you on Saturday?"

Emma hesitated for a fraction of a second before she answered. "Mark and I will come alone," she decided. "That's the point of the exercise. Jet is to be a great surprise for Harry – a sort of joint surprise," she added as they reached the door. "He adores Mark, as you can imagine, but he doesn't know about Jet. Not yet!" The dark eyes glowed with pride in her son. "I want Harry to grow up in a free atmosphere, close to nature, and Mark thinks the same."

Obviously Mark Bradley was the ideal of the man she wanted most to influence her child. Ruth watched her remount her horse and ride off, an upright, elegant figure in her immaculate riding-clothes with her face turned to the sun.

It was well into the afternoon before Becky reappeared at Lovesome Hill.

"Where, in heaven's name, have you been all this time?" Ruth demanded.

"In Derham."

"For four hours?"

The colour rose in Becky's cheeks. "I met someone. We had a snack together at the Three Tuns."

50

"Who?" Ruth asked as Becky didn't seem to be as forthcoming as usual.

"Tim Spurrier."

"The name doesn't ring a bell," Ruth decided.

"He's a groom up at High Parks. We've met once or twice while he's been exercising Mark Bradley's horses on the high moor," Becky explained almost reluctantly. "He's not a local."

"What else is wrong with him?" Ruth asked teasingly.

"There's nothing wrong with him," Becky assured her, depositing her purchases on the deal table in the kitchen. "He's just a bit more – reserved than the others and he's as keen as mustard to be a successful jockey one day."

"Becky," Ruth pointed out, "having two strings to your bow can only lead to trouble, especially in a small place like Derham."

"You mean Chay Oliver, don't you?" her sister challenged. "Well, he's years older than me and terribly – staid." She considered the word for a moment. "Yes – staid. That's it! I don't want to be stuck in a rut up here for the rest of my life."

"You'll hardly be doing that at university," Ruth pointed out quietly.

"I'm not going back to York," Becky protested. "I've told you!"

Ruth grasped the edge of the table. "Have you told Mother?" she demanded.

"No."

"Well, don't. Not until you've thought more carefully about it."

"If you're hoping I'll change my mind you're mistaken." Becky looked round the tidy kitchen. "I'm not at all like you. I'm not cut out for domestic bliss. I've got to be free – free to do my own thing," she added determinedly.

Before Ruth could answer she had slammed the communicating door into the hall and gone off to her own room.

When Ruth finally told her about Emma Falconer's visit, however, their brief disagreement was immediately forgotten.

"That's super!" she declared. "When will they come for Jet?"

"We arranged for Saturday afternoon," Ruth told her. "Mark Bradley is lending – or giving – her a horse-box for the journey to the Grange."

"Is he coming with her?" Becky demanded, immediately interested.

"I think so."

"There's a lot of speculation about them locally," Becky told her. "Tim say they've been friends for years, as far as he can gather, but Mark Bradley's just not interested in women. Tim says he lives up at High Parks alone because he's had a bad experience of love and can't forget it."

"Tim Gossip!" Ruth scoffed. "Maybe he should find something better to do."

The fact that Mark did live at High Parks alone certainly intrigued the village worthies who declared that he should have left the Stone Birds where he had found them in the ditch and not built two great monoliths for them to sit on and bring him bad luck in love or anything else.

Becky made a point of being on hand all morning on the following Saturday, lingering in the paddock to say goodbye to the first love of her life.

"You'll be happy, Jet," she kept repeating. "You're going to a little boy who'll take you out every day and love you very much."

It was hardly enough reassurance for Jet as his great, sad eyes questioned hers and his soft nose nuzzled

52

lovingly into her neck. 'Don't desert me,' he appealed. 'I'm happy enough with you.'

Mark Bradley drove into the cobbled yard at eleven o'clock, towing a small horse-box behind his car. He was alone. Becky rushed out to meet him.

"You've come for Jet," she said, holding back the tears. "I'll just get him – something to eat on the way."

She left Mark standing with his cheque in his hand as he looked about him with interest and Ruth felt obliged to welcome him.

"Will you come inside?" she asked. "Parting is never an easy thing when it comes to an animal you've loved."

"Agreed." He strode across the yard by her side, a tall man not easily disturbed by emotion. "Becky needn't worry," he said. "She'll be made welcome at the Grange whenever she likes to come."

The brief remark seemed to underline his association with the Grange and its new owner, but he made no further reference to Emma as he paid his respects to Hester who had come to the back door to bid him welcome.

"You'll come in for something to drink," she offered. "I'm brewing up some coffee and trying to make myself useful. A body gets tired just sitting around while everyone else is up to their elbows in hard work."

Mark looked across the kitchen at Ruth. "I hear you're getting ready for the sorting," he observed. "Have you extra help?"

Ruth shook her head, conscious of the fact that Emma must have told him about their encounter at the barn.

"I can manage," she declared. "Amos – our shepherd – has promised to come back in an emergency and there's always Becky."

He did not make any reference to Becky's worth. "If you need help," he said, and left it there.

It was a long time before Becky came in from the

53

paddock. "Jet's ready," she said, holding back the tears. "Will you take him quickly, please?"

Mark rose to his feet, looking down at the neat pile of blankets she had placed on the table before him.

"You may need these for another horse," he suggested. "One more suited to you size than Jet."

Becky sighed. "No – you take them. I won't be having a horse of my own for some time," she told him. "I'll just have to ride other people's."

"If you need an occasional mount I could find you one at High Parks," Mark suggested.

The offer took Becky's breath away. "Do you mean that?" she gasped. "Are you saying I could sometimes ride for you?"

"Not professionally," he told her, "unless I tried you out first."

"I'm a good rider," Becky assured him eagerly. "I've had lots of practice, especially on the moors. I could fill in for you if you ever found yourself short of a groom."

Mark passed over his cheque, laying it on the table beside the blankets.

"At the moment I have more lads than I need," he said briefly, "but if anything should change I'll let you know."

Becky had to be content with that, but there was a high colour in her cheeks and a gleam in her eyes as she went ahead to the paddock where an expectant little pony was waiting for her.

Ruth could hardly credit what she had just heard. Mark Bradley half-promising Becky a job. It was unbelievable.

"You could have thought that out more carefully," she told him, unable to hide her annoyance. "We need Becky's help here, such as it is. With the sortings beginning next week I'll be out on the hill most days and if you know anything about hill farming that means practically from

54

dawn to dusk. Becky will be needed in the house to look after my mother and do the cooking."

"My humble apologies!" She could not quite read the expression in his eyes. "I must have thought you had more help in the house."

"I manage," Ruth assured him, hoping that he didn't think she was appealing for his sympathy. "Normally there would be no problem but someone's got to be on the hill."

He stood looking at her for a moment longer before he finally turned away. Becky was leading a reluctant Jet towards the horse-box and he went round the back to let down the ramp.

Jet went meekly with one last glance at Becky, who was now in tears.

"I shouldn't have sold him," she gulped. "Not for all the tea in China!"

Ruth put a comforting arm about her shoulders. "Mrs Falconer said you could visit at the Grange whenever you like," she consoled. "It was a promise."

"I don't think I could bear to see Jet again," Becky said. "I'd want him back."

"Don't take it too hard," Ruth consoled. "Jet is too small for you now and he's going to someone who will love him. Mrs Falconer's son seems to be a lonely little boy in need of companionship so Jet will be just right for him."

"Harry," Becky said. "I think he's been quite sickly when he was little and Mrs Falconer thinks the life up here will do him the world of good. She appears to depend on Mark for advice rather a lot," she added half-resentfully. "Do you think they're lovers?"

"I don't know," Ruth said. "And does it really matter? She's a widow and he's free, apparently – free to admire anyone he likes."

"She's older than he is, don't you think?" Becky suggested.

"Not so very much. Perhaps a year or two. It isn't significant," Ruth said. "They both appear to love Harry and that's all that matters."

"I don't think they're right for each other," Becky objected. "She's too – passive, too correct. You could imagine sparks flying with someone with a bit of spunk if they crossed Mark Bradley and it might be fun to try. What do you think?"

"If you are really asking for my advice," Ruth said a trifle sharply, "I wouldn't risk the encounter. You would be sure to come off second best."

"You think?" Becky said. "All the same, I mean to try. I mean to strike up a friendship if I possibly can."

A week later the sortings began. The sheep were driven down from the high moor to be collected into pens where each farmer identified his own for shearing in due course. A few sheep had been left nearer the farms, late-born lambs and sickly ewes who might have fared badly on the wide, open spaces of the moor. Lovesome Hill had only a handful of these problem creatures and Ruth had been checking on them personally since her return. So far she had not encountered any trouble, but in the middle of the week a local farmhand drove up to tell her that one of her flock needed her attention.

"There's one o' your beasts down in the far meadow," he called without shutting off the engine of his car. "Ah'd help, but Ah'm off tae Harrogate on an errand for t' boss. Better get thissen up there as soon as tha' can."

Ruth wasted no time. As usual, Becky was nowhere to be seen and she explained the emergency to Hester as best she could.

"One of the tups is in trouble in the far meadow so I'm

56

off up there to see what's wrong. It can't be very much. I had a look at them yesterday. Becky can see to the dinner when she comes in."

"I'll do the potatoes," Hester offered. "Don't worry about the meal."

Dressed for action in washed-out jeans and a blue sweater, Ruth drove swiftly to the far meadow. It was a lovely day, warm with sunshine and no wind. Not even the grasses stirred as she parked her car in the meadow gateway to look at the flock. All seemed well until she noticed the late-born lamb they had nurtured from birth at Lovesome Hill, bottle-feeding him in front of the Aga before he was put out into the paddock beside Jet for a week or two. Steady on his legs at last, he had been transferred to the far meadow where he was eventually accepted by the ewes who had inhabited it before him.

When Ruth finally reached him he was lying on his back, eyes fixed in a terrifying stare. "Up you get!" she commanded. "There can't be much wrong with you. You were all over the field yesterday making a nuisance of yourself."

The other occupants of the meadow stood around anxiously as she rolled the heavy lamb over to examine him. She could find nothing wrong, but the lamb collapsed again when he attempted to stand. I'll have to carry him, she thought; there's nothing else for it.

She had climbed quite high up the sloping meadow to reach her objective and it seemed a very long way back to the gate and her waiting car, but there was no alternative.

Well fed for the past two months, the lamb was no light burden and presently she began to struggle under his weight. Ruth set him down among the grasses while she drew breath.

"You are a problem," she said aloud. "You always

were, but we have to see what's wrong with you. If you hadn't eaten so much you wouldn't be so heavy."

The lamb bleated back at her, looking pathetic.

It was then that she realized that they were no longer alone. The tall figure of a man was approaching through the grasses and her heart gave a bound as she recognized Mark Bradley.

"In trouble?" he enquired, standing above her knee-deep in meadow grass and buttercups. "Can I help?"

Ruth straightened, unable to conceal her surprise.

"How did you get here?" she asked. "There's rarely anyone around at this time of day."

"I was coming back from Leeds," he said, bending to inspect the lamb. "What do you think has gone wrong?"

"I wish I knew," Ruth told him, mopping her brow. "I'm not an expert. I'll have to get back to the house and call the vet."

"Let me have a look." He ran his long fingers gently along the lamb's back, probing expertly, lifting each extended leg in turn before he laid the strong little animal back on the grass at her feet. "We'll take him back to the farm," he decided. "Better safe than sorry."

Gently he lifted the lamb onto his shoulders, striding ahead of her down the grassy slope. It all appeared to be so easy, Ruth thought, although the lamb was no lightweight. The gentleness in him was a great surprise to her because she had considered him hard in the extreme.

"I can't thank you enough," she said when they had reached the gate. "That would have taken me ages."

"We'll get him into my truck," he suggested. "He could make a mess of your car."

"Really, I can manage," Ruth objected almost automatically. "There's a rug in the back of the car."

He turned to look down at her. "Don't argue," he said.

"There's far more room in the truck and no way of a rampant lamb interfering with my steering."

"If you're sure—"

"I'm quite sure, otherwise I wouldn't have offered." He laid the lamb down between two bales of straw which he had probably collected at a nearby farm on his way from the city. "Try not to be so independent, especially in an emergency."

The lamb settled happily against the straw and Mark turned to see her into her car.

"You don't know anything about me," he said when Ruth suggested that it was going to take him out of his way. "You've heard how I live up there at High Parks like a recluse and you're not going to feel 'obliged' for any help I might offer you. That's the truth, isn't it?" He fixed her with a compelling stare. "You don't like taking people at face value when you believe they might double-cross you – especially a man."

A tell-tale colour flamed in Ruth's cheeks. "I don't make friends easily," she conceded, "if that's what you mean."

"I had come to that conclusion," he said, "but we did shake hands on a truce."

She remembered the touch of his long, lean fingers on hers and the way his lips had curved in a wry smile as he had let them go. Was it true that he would never trust a woman no matter how honest she might seem? His friendship with Emma Falconer seemed to deny this. Their close friendship.

It was less than a mile to Lovesome Hill and she followed him slowly to find the truck parked at the paddock gate.

"We'll leave him where he is," he said, looking down at the recumbent lamb. "He looks comfortable enough, but I'll stand by till you contact the vet."

Ruth nodded. It seemed that the whole event had been taken out of her hands.

When she phoned the surgery Chay Oliver had just come in.

"I'll be with you in ten minutes," he assured her. "No sweat!"

"Chay's coming right away," she told Mark. "We can always rely on him. You must want to get away," she suggested. "We could move the lamb into the paddock."

"I'd leave well alone, if I were you," he returned. "A sick animal is often best left where he is comfortable till you get an expert on the job."

"You handled him well." She was truly grateful. "You seem to have a way with animals."

"I've worked with them for most of my life."

He was still reticent about his past and she would not try to force a confidence. Whatever he had been, wherever he had worked before coming to High Parks, was entirely his own affair, she told herself determinedly.

"I could offer you some tea," she said, "if you would like to come up to the house?"

He shook his head. "I won't disturb your mother. I know she rests in the afternoon. Where's Becky?" he asked.

"Out somewhere. She's going to have plenty to do next week in the house so she's taking the afternoon off, I expect."

"What about you?"

Ruth laughed. "I won't have any time off till the hay is cut and the shearing is out of the way," she said. "After all, I came back to make myself useful and that's what I'll do."

"Supposing your ancient shepherd doesn't turn up?" he asked.

"Oh – Amos! He'll keep his word all right."

"He's far too old to be working on the hill."

"Shepherds are never too old. As long as they can stand up they'll be out there tending the sheep," Ruth assured him. "They'll grumble, of course – they always do, especially after an accident – but it's their life and they wouldn't do anything else, believe me. I thought we were going to be without Amos for a while but he's offered to help out as much as he can." She ran her fingers along the side of the truck. "It's better than nothing," she decided. "Another pair of hands."

He stood looking down at the lamb nestling in the hay. "Will you make me a promise?" he asked.

"Another one!"

"I'm serious, Ruth. I want to make sure you'll ask for help if you really need it."

She felt the colour rise in her cheeks, but she did not refuse him this time. "I'll keep you in mind," she said. "It's – very kind of you."

Again she saw the wry smile curve his sensitive mouth, but this time there was no cynicism about it. He really did want to help and, after all, that was what the whole dale was about. Nobody went short of assistance while a neighbour could lend a hand and she supposed she would do the same for him.

Strange how a sickly lamb on a sunlit hillside could alter her whole conception of a man; strange how she had imagined him so hostile when they had first met!

The sound of a hesitant engine chugging up the hill suggested that the vet had arrived. Chay Oliver climbed out of his ancient Vauxhall after he drew up behind Ruth's car.

"Having trouble?" he asked.

"Not too much, I hope." Ruth introduced him to Mark. "It's Bambi," she added. "You know, Becky's poorly lamb. He's been out in the far meadow with the others but

61

now, suddenly, his legs have given way. It's disappointing because I thought he had grown quite tough."

"I'll have a look at him. Where's Becky?" Chay asked, glancing behind them at the house. "I saw her in Derham yesterday." He glanced sideways in Mark's direction. "She was riding a black yearling up towards the gallops. Something she had borrowed, I suppose."

"She didn't say." Ruth was too concerned about his patient to pay much attention to her sister's movements at the moment. "She usually borrows a mount from the Metcalfs and they've got more than one horse. Was Kate with her?"

"No." Chay shook his head, his natural ruddy colouring deepening as he bent into the back of the truck. "No, she wasn't. It was a stranger – a man," he added shamefacedly.

Mark stood aside to let him examine the lamb.

"I'm going up to the house to make some tea," Ruth said, "and I'm not taking any refusals," she added, looking directly at Mark.

He was frowning, a dark anger in his eyes making them hard as flint. "You must excuse me," he said. "I've got something important to do in Derham which I can't put off."

Disappointed, Ruth turned away. Unashamedly she had hoped for his company for a little longer, hoped to get to know him better, perhaps, but now he had clamped up on her as coldly as before, refusing a simple offer of hospitality which she thought he deserved.

He stayed talking to Chay for another ten minutes, discussing the lamb, no doubt, before he drove away.

"It's nothing serious," Chay assured her when he came to the kitchen door. "He's been putting on an act – playing for sympathy when he got tired of being one of the flock instead of an individual. They're sly creatures are lambs, wiser than you'd think when a nice convenient bottle of milk comes to mind. You could feed him for a day or two up here and then take him back to the flock where he'll eventually settle down. I'll leave you these." He put a small bottle of pills down on the kitchen table. "One in each feed in case it is a touch of rheumatism," he added.

"You'll stay for a meal?" Hester suggested, hobbling through from the sitting-room at the sound of their voices. "You'll be more than welcome."

Chay hesitated. "I've two more calls to make," he said regretfully. "Perhaps another time."

After he had gone Hester stood at the open door looking out across the yard to the field barn where the swallows were darting, circling and sweeping in the fading sunlight on their first foray of the evening. She often stood there at this time of day, her eyes wistful as she looked across the meadows to the green slopes of the hills where the wind blew strongest. Yeomen farmers had built their sturdy stone farmhouses here in the nineteenth century, surrounding their fields with miles of dry-stone walling along the lower slopes and dotting the valley with the stone field barns which could be seen for miles. It was her country. A farmer's daughter, she could look back to a long line of ancestors who had farmed the land and bred cattle and herded sheep not too far away from Lovesome Hill. She knew it all so well, the flat, deeply creviced limestone pavements on the ice-sculptured hilltops, the dramatic waterfalls and the warrens of the potholes were familiar ground to her which she would never have thought of leaving for an easier life elsewhere.

"Four summers now," she said to Ruth who came to stand beside her, "I've watched the swallows come back to their old nests in the field barns, flying half-way across the world to come home."

Ruth knew that her mother's heart was still full of hope that one day Jonathan would return, so how could she tell her that she could only think of him as already dead?

"Come in," she said, putting a gentle hand on her stooped shoulders. "There's no use you getting cold."

The sortings meant that everything else had to be put aside. Ruth forgot about Becky riding a strange black horse up onto the gallops while she made her way with Amos up onto the moor. They were not alone. Most of the dale farmers were herding the sheep down into the sorting pens where they were divided carefully according to their different marks. It took days and she was too tired by nightfall to even wonder about Becky's riding companion.

Becky, too, was strangely quiet and little disposed to a confidence. She prepared meals and baked bread under Hester's tuition, seemingly reasonably content.

"I suppose when all this is over we can get down to some partying," she suggested when the last of the sheep were off the hill. "You're coming to the barbecue, I suppose?"

"Nothing would hold me back!" Ruth smiled, wondering if Mark would be there.

She hadn't seen him for over a week and it seemed a very long time.

"You'll be going with Chay?" she asked. "You always do."

Becky hesitated. "I'm not sure," she said. "I have someone else in my sights."

"Not Henry Metcalf!" Ruth teased. "He'd tread on your toes."

"I wasn't thinking about Henry," Becky told her.

"Who, then?"

"Someone else I've met," Becky confided carefully.

"Tim Spurrier, as a matter of fact. We have so much in common and he's even let me ride his horse."

Ruth was halted in her tracks, remembering what Chay had said about seeing her sister riding with a stranger in Derham and Mark's swift reaction to the fact.

"Becky, if he's only a groom it can't possibly be *his* horse!" she countered.

"He won't be 'only a groom' for long," Becky declared defensively. "He's got lots of ambition and Mark Bradley seems to trust him."

"That won't last if he is letting you ride Mark's horses," Ruth warned. "And I wasn't suggesting that a groom is in any way inferior. It's not that. It's a matter of trust. Mark wouldn't expect anyone to be riding his horse if they were not fully trained."

"I'm a good rider!" Becky protested. "Better than most, and even Mark Bradley will have to acknowledge that. Anyway, he said he'd let me have a horse to ride any time I wanted one if I went to High Parks."

"And asked his permission," Ruth pointed out. "Which I suppose you haven't done."

"I didn't see any need to ask," Becky protested, "and what he doesn't know won't worry him too much."

"Becky!" Ruth protested. "That's plain stupid. Supposing you had an accident?"

"I don't have accidents." Becky's confidence was in full flow. "I've been riding practically all my life."

"A pony!" Ruth exclaimed. "There's no comparison."

Should she tell Becky that Mark was already aware of her little adventure on the moor? Well, perhaps not, since it would involve Chay, who was anything but a gossip. Mark would sort it out for himself.

"You don't understand," Becky was accusing her. "It's

Mark Bradley's horse, of course, but Tim rides it all the time. They're up at the gallops every day."

"I can't believe you're telling me this!" Ruth exclaimed. "Tim Spurrier must be mad to allow you to ride a potential racehorse that could be very valuable."

"He's not stupid," Becky declared. "He's there all the time. He's an excellent rider."

"I'm not disputing that," Ruth said. "It's the clandestine way you are going about it that bothers me."

"Because you've got Mark Bradley's interests at heart," Becky challenged, "and you don't want your sister putting a spoke in your wheel where he's concerned?"

Ruth flushed. "That's not true," she cried. "I hardly know Mark and he doesn't make friends easily as far as I can gather."

"Only at Winterside Grange," Becky suggested. "He's there all the time, according to Tim."

Ruth's heart gave a sharp lurch of disappointment although she had already accepted the fact that Mark was no stranger at the Grange. "I'm not going to argue any more," she declared. "I've said my piece and it's up to you now – and Tim Spurrier. I don't know him, but I think he'll be sensible enough if you tell him you don't want to ride again without Mark's permission."

"Which wouldn't be true," Becky returned, striding off in the direction of the barn.

Differences of opinion didn't last very long at Lovesome Hill, however, and by nightfall they were discussing what they should wear at the Metcalfs' barbecue the following evening.

"Could I borrow your blue skirt?" Becky asked. "It would go nicely with my blouse. Which I haven't ironed yet!" she remembered. "I'll do it in the morning," she decided. "What are you going to wear?"

Ruth considered the question. "Something suitable,"

she decided in her turn. "I know what barbecues are like. A blouse and skirt, I suppose. Probably the blue one," she teased.

"Why don't you wear that cotton frock with the lace collar?" Becky suggested. "Green suits you."

"Green it is, then," Ruth agreed. "I'll take something warm to cover up with if it gets cold."

They would be dancing in the Metcalfs' barn and she was looking forward to it. Not only because Mark Bradley might be there, she tried to assure herself but because it was the first opportunity she had had to relax and really enjoy herself since her return to the dale.

Working with the sheep had roughened her hands and she rubbed moisturing cream into them before she dressed. The green cotton frock lay on her bed, the colour, patterned with tiny daisy-heads, made her think of the far meadow and Mark coming to her rescue with the lamb. He had been all tenderness as he had carried it back to the road, amazing her even as she thought about him again. Yet she had looked into eyes as grey as slate when he had heard about her sister's clandestine adventures on the moor. His anger would be devastating, she thought, wondering how Becky could have been so foolish, even after he had offered her a mount.

When she came down the stairs for her mother's inspection Becky was already there.

"You're looking grand, the pair of you!" Hester smiled. "I suppose I needn't expect you back before tomorrow morning."

"We'll be safe enough," Becky assured her. "You know the Metcalfs!"

"And I know all about barbecues, although we used to call them plain Barn Dances in my day," Hester said. "Have you enough petrol in the car?"

"More than enough," Ruth assured her, kissing her goodbye. "You'll be all right?"

"As safe as houses," Hester answered. "Off you go and enjoy yourselves!"

Proudly she looked after her daughters, thinking how blessed she was.

Ruth drove swiftly along the winding dale road towards Derham, crossing the Wade bridge which spanned the turbulent Dere above the falls. Like most dale settlements Derham was built high, its houses stepping down to the river in their own cascade of weathered stone, its cobbled square forming a central heart from which narrow lanes led away to hidden courtyards steeped in endless time. Bronze and Iron Age settlements had fashioned the townships; a king had built himself a castle on a hill and the Iron Age Brigantes had defended it successfully against the Romans. Ruth had always felt the sense of history unfolding around them, but Becky was a child of today.

"We're late," she said. "Later than we promised."

Conscious of not making any promises, Ruth parked the car in the sloping cobbled square. The Metcalfs owned the local grocery store amongst other businesses. Their house was straight across the square from the shop, a two-storeyed Georgian residence with a rather ostentatious flagpole jutting out from above the front door which was seldom used. They also farmed on the far side of the dale, where they bred pigs for their famous bacon, but the Derham house was their real home. Ruth drove under a wide stone archway to the more familiar rear of the house where the barbecue was in full progress.

"Everybody's here," Becky said, looking around her at the assembled company as Kate Metcalf came to meet them.

"You're late," she said. "Come on in, Ruth!"

She was a tall, angular girl with no pretence at beauty, her hair usually worn in a tight plait behind her head, but her brown eyes were amazingly kind. Ruth had known her for twenty years. Tonight her hair was loosened, falling in a golden-brown cascade about her shoulders and held in place by a brown velvet band.

"Are we expecting someone special?" Becky asked cruelly.

Kate flushed. "I'm trying to look my best," she smiled without taking umbrage. "The only 'special' person I can think of is Mark Bradley. Mother thought we should invite him."

She hadn't abandoned her usual jeans although she had paired them with an elaborate new sweater which came down to her knees. Needing the extra length, she had rolled up the too-long sleeves, exposing her bony arms which were entirely devoid of jewellery, except for a man's practical watch.

"Mark Bradley," Becky said. "Has he arrived?"

"Not yet," Kate said. "But he did promise when Mother phoned."

"I'll be surprised if he turns up," Becky decided. "He's completely unpredictable."

Kate led the way across a stepped terrace to where most of her guests were gathered around the barbecue grill. It was glowing red now though a whiff of smoke still lingered in the air above their heads. Henry Metcalf, a tall, raw-boned teenager, was busy turning chicken thighs over on the grill where steaks and sausages were already being served.

"Hi!" he greeted them. "You're late. Did you have a puncture on the way?"

"Of course not! Ruth looks after her car." Becky was gazing round for someone she knew. "Where's everyone?"

"Mostly in the barn." Henry turned his attention back to the grill. "That chap you know from High Parks has turned up. I forget his name."

"Tim," Becky said. "Tim Spurrier."

"He's an odd sort of bloke," Henry observed. "Doesn't have a lot to say."

"It depends who he's speaking to."

Becky moved along the terrace with a charred steak and a jacket potato on her plate, leaving Ruth to wonder who had really invited her sister's new acquaintance. If Mark had also been invited there might be fireworks, although she suspected that Mark's anger was more likely to be a cold, determined thing.

In the barn a good many people were already dancing. She saw Becky with Tim Spurrier and drew in a deep breath. He was good-looking enough but desperately thin, and he had the same determined cut to his jaw as she remembered in Mark, making it almost inevitable that they would clash. Mark, of course, would come out the winner because this time he would be in the right. He would hold the whip hand, but she thought he would also be fair.

Kate Metcalf came to stand beside her.

"I'm glad you could come, Ruth," she said, genuinely pleased. "It's like old times. Remember how we used to sit on the stairs and look down at the dancers when we weren't supposed to be there? Then, after we went to dancing class we could both join in. I was the awkward one, of course, while you were always popular. You never needed to bring a partner, although Jon was always there to bring you home." Suddenly her brown eyes clouded over. "You've heard nothing, of course?" she added.

"No." Ruth gazed down at her fingertips. "It isn't the same, is it? One of us missing. If we could only be sure he's alive that would be something. Jon was always the life and soul of your parties. You must miss him, too."

Kate's firm lips trembled a little. "More than you know," she confessed. "I keep telling myself that he couldn't just go away like that for good, but it's no use. These things happen." She straightened the wrist-watch on her bony arm. "Have a charred steak," she invited. "Henry gets over-enthusiastic when he's in charge of the grill. I'm glad you made it, Ruth," she added more seriously. "You look lovely. You always do."

Ruth smiled, knowing the compliment to be genuine. Kate had always been frank with her, even in the last part of their schooldays when she had been sent off to Harrogate 'to become a lady' and Ruth had stayed behind at the local secondary school.

"I see Becky has a new beau," Kate observed, looking across the barn to where Becky was feeding Tim Spurrier potato from her own plate. "He looks in need of a decent meal. Have you met him?"

"Not yet. Not officially," Ruth confessed. "He's a groom up at High Parks, I gather."

"And Becky will use him for her own ends," Kate decided. "At least till the summer is over. I've offered her the use of a horse to ride any time, but it seems my old hacks are not really what she wants."

"Kate, that's what worries me," Ruth confessed. "She talks about riding professionally and you know that's not on. It would break my mother's heart if she gave up university now."

"No doubt she'll see the light come September," Kate suggested. "We all go through this silly stage, more or less."

"You didn't," Ruth declared. "You knew what you wanted to do right from the beginning."

Kate looked beyond her. "Did I?" she said. "Did I really have any choice?"

Her father came towards them, playing the benevolent host. A big, fleshy man, he had a ribald sense of humour and a particularly glassy stare when he imagined that he was being thwarted. He had built up a considerable business in the small market town, starting off with a grocery store and soon branching out in other directions to eventually own a large sadlery shop and a thriving restaurant. 'You can get anything you need at Metcalfs' and even more' had been his motto for the past thirty years and it had never been fully challenged. Smaller shops had sprung up around him only to be out of business within a year because he was able to undercut their prices and survive.

"Are you back for good?" he asked Ruth bluntly. "It's what you should have done a year ago. Your mother took on far too much up there at Lovesome Hill when your father died. He was a man after my own heart," he reminisced. "Always sure of what he had to do. It's a pity that brother of yours didn't take after him, eh? He would have been here now to take his share of the burden. His rightful share."

"We don't consider it a burden," Ruth said. "Certainly I'm happy to do all I can for Lovesome Hill."

"Who's this fellow young Becky's got in tow?" William Metcalf demanded. "I see him riding a nice bit of horseflesh up on the moor from time to time."

"He's a groom at High Parks," his daughter told him. "Ruth hasn't met him yet."

"A groom?" William sucked in his lips. "What's she up to?" he wanted to know.

"Becky wants to ride professionally," Kate told him, "but somebody ought to put a stop to that. It will only end in grief."

"She's got plenty of spunk in her," William said. "You have to admit that. When she was only knee-high to a grasshopper she could ride like the wind on that pony of hers. Has she still got it?"

"She's grown out of Jet," Ruth told him. "She sold him to the people at the Grange."

William's eyes twinkled. "Oh, ay?" he remarked. "She's a bonnie widow, that one. I spoke to her the other day and invited her over here and she said she couldn't promise but she would try." He looked down the long barn. "She hasn't put in an appearance yet so I reckon she has better things to do. I hear she's pretty thick with our new neighbour up at High Parks." He looked at Ruth, his small eyes quizzical in his flushed red face. "What do you think?" he asked.

"I wouldn't know," Ruth returned as calmly as possible. "I don't know Mark Bradley well enough to discuss his private affairs."

"And you wouldn't even if you did!" William chortled. "Good for you! You're your mother's daughter all right."

With that he left them, lumbering across the barn to greet his latest guest.

"I wish my father would mind his own business," Kate said. "I'm sorry if he embarrassed you, Ruth."

"Asking what I knew about Mark Bradley." Ruth forced a smile. "It was natural enough, I suppose."

"It was downright curiosity. At one time he thought of buying High Parks himself, but I think the legend eventually deterred him," Kate laughed. "He's highly superstitious, you know, and the thought of the Stone Birds' curse put him off."

"What would he have done with it?" Ruth wanted to know. "High Parks, I mean."

"Moved us all up there to appear grander than we really are," Kate answered without rancour. "It would have killed my mother to have moved so far away from her roots in Derham. As it is she seldom goes to the farm and she hates it when the pigs are killed. She never eats bacon."

"I love your mother. Always have," Ruth said. "She never complains."

Kate shrugged. "If she did it would get her nowhere," she decided, moving away to receive another guest.

Ruth knew that she was waiting for Mark to put in an appearance. She had hoped that he would come, deep down for no apparent reason, but still there was no sign of him.

Eventually Becky brought her dancing partner over to say 'Hello'.

"This is Tim," she introduced him.

Tim Spurrier shook Ruth by the hand. "Pleased to meet you," he said almost painfully. "Do you dance?"

"I've been known to," Ruth said, still looking for Mark among the crowd at the door.

"Would you like to?" Tim asked.

She could hardly refuse, Ruth thought as he edged her onto the floor. His body was like a thin steel rod under the checked shirt he wore and she felt that there could not be any flesh on him at all. He had hollow cheeks and great dark eyes and he breathed heavily as they circled the floor. Trying to make conversation was difficult, but she did her best.

"You don't belong around here," she suggested. "Are you from farther north?"

"No – south," he said, sounding awkward.

"You like the work you're doing?"

"Oh, yeah!" he said. "I've a good opportunity here."

"You won't have if you betray Mr Bradley's trust," Ruth found herself saying bluntly.

"I don't know what you mean."

"I think you do, Tim," Ruth said. "Becky shouldn't be riding one of his horses without his permission. You must know that."

His thin frame stiffened. "She's not doing any harm," he said between his teeth.

"Think about it," Ruth said. "It could all end unhappily if Mr Bradley found out. As a matter of fact, I think he already knows."

It was a warning she felt she had to make, more for Becky's sake than anything else.

Tim led her back to her seat, neither promising to take her words to heart nor to disregard them out of hand. She was getting nowhere with him, Ruth decided. Now it would depend upon what Mark would do.

It was past midnight before she saw him standing in the doorway of the brightly lit barn and he was not alone. Emma Falconer was by his side, dressed discreetly in a pale, rose-coloured kaftan which Ruth guessed had cost a lot of money.

Swiftly Kate moved towards them. "They've come, after all," she said.

Ruth turned away, knowing that she had been waiting for Mark all evening. At the far end of the barn he was greeting Kate and introducing Emma; then he was dancing with Kate and then with Emma while Ruth was swept up in a rowdy square dance which seemed to have no beginning and no end as far as she was concerned. All she could see was Mark's dark head and Emma's sculptured chignon close together, seeming to shut out everyone else. She tried to tell herself that it was madness to think like this about someone she scarcely knew, madness to even consider that Mark would want to dance with her, but it did not keep her foolish heart from hoping.

After he had danced with Kate for a second time and Emma had been swept away in someone else's arms he sat down beside William Metcalf and began to talk. They had obviously met before and it seemed to Ruth that he would stay in Bill Metcalf's company for the remainder of the evening.

Turning, she found Chay Oliver by her side. "Dance?" he asked, trying not to look in Becky's direction.

"I'd like a drink of lemonade," Ruth said.

The veterinary rushed to obtain her request from the bar set up at the far end of the barn while she tried not to look too often at the bench where Bill Metcalf sat with his latest guest.

"Do we dance or just sit this one out?" a well-remembered voice asked behind her. "I warn you I'm not exactly an expert."

She turned to look at Mark, thinking how cool he was and how assured.

"We don't," she said stiffly. "Dance, I mean. Chay Oliver has already asked me."

"Ah – the vet," he said. "I saw him heading for the bar."

"To bring me a lemonade. I felt thirsty."

He sat down in the chair beside hers. "No need to explain," he said. "I thought it only polite to ask and then to warn you about my lack of the social graces."

"I don't believe you can't dance," she said, angry that a hot colour was rising in her cheeks. "I saw you a moment ago."

"With Emma," he laughed. "But Emma puts up with all my limitations. We have been friends for years."

She switched the conversations deliberately. "Is she quite pleased with Jet?" she asked, wondering why Chay was taking so long to fetch a humble glass of lemonade.

"She's enchanted. I couldn't have chosen better even if I had tried a lot harder," Mark informed her. "Jet was just

76

waiting for us. Harry, of course, thinks he's the best pony that ever walked around on four legs. We've christened him Beauty. Do you mind?"

"Jet was never my pony," Ruth said. "He has always belonged to Becky."

"Ah – Becky!" His eyes suddenly narrowed. "I wanted a word with her. She's somewhere around, I suppose."

"She was out at the barbecue when I last saw her." A lump had risen in Ruth's throat which was something like fear. "About her riding one of your horses," she forced herself to say. "I don't think she meant any harm."

"No?"

The cold monosyllable made her turn to look at him and all she could see in his face was anger.

"Let me – speak to her about it," she suggested. "She knows she's doing wrong."

"She could kill herself." His mouth had clamped into an unforgiving line. "That horse isn't fully trained yet and he's a bundle of fire and unpredictability. Into the bargain he has a sullen temper which hasn't yet been curbed."

"Don't blame Becky too much," she begged. "She's always been horse mad."

"Ruth," he said in a gentler tone, "you're taking on far too much responsibility for that sister of yours. She'll twist you round her little finger and be damned to you."

"You don't really know her," Ruth said. "She's very loyal in spite of going off at a tangent occasionally. I wouldn't want you to – threaten her in any way."

Suddenly he looked amused. "I might have expected you to say something like that," he told her. "I'll bear it in mind. 'Don't be too hard on my sister because she's really very sweet.' That was about the gist of it, wasn't it?"

"If you like," Ruth said. "All I'm asking is that you let me talk to her again before you bawl her out."

"Again?" he queried.

Ruth bit her lip. "I have pointed out how foolish she is being, but it takes time to sink in where Becky is concerned. She isn't always so—"

"Thrawn," he supplied. "But is that too Scottish a word for you?"

"I know what it means," Ruth agreed. "Were you never unduly stubborn yourself?"

"Plenty of times." He dismissed Becky's problem with a brief gesture. "But here comes your refreshment and your dancing partner. Maybe I could have the dance after next?"

It was a suggestion she was not supposed to refuse, Ruth thought as she took to the floor with Chay Oliver, but an announcement by their younger host took her by surprise as she returned to the chairs where they had been sitting.

"Sorry," Henry said almost sheepishly, "but we have an old-fashioned waltz now. My mother's choice."

Ruth looked at her watch. It was five minutes to two. Bleak disappointment clouded her vision.

"Henry must mean it's the last waltz." She met Mark's eyes with a steady resolve in her own. "You must want to dance it with Mrs Falconer," she suggested.

Mark looked across the barn to where Emma Falconer was still deep in conversation with William Metcalf.

"Why should I?" he asked. "Emma likes to talk more than she likes to dance. Besides, I asked you."

Without further argument he put his arm around her waist, guiding her purposefully onto the dance floor.

"You lied when you said you couldn't dance," she accused him when they had circled the barn twice. "You waltz very well."

For a moment he didn't answer her. "It all comes back to you after a while," he said at last. "I was taught by an expert, you see."

His voice was suddenly harsh and when she looked up at him his mouth was grim. His thoughts had gone back into the past, as her own so often did, and they were not happy ones.

Well, the dance was nearly over and she would enjoy what was left of it! Mark's arm tightened about her. They were close now, closer than convention demanded, and she could feel the hard strength of his body through the thin cotton dress covered in the white daisies which reminded her so vividly of their brief encounter up there in the far meadow when he had come to the rescue of the lamb.

The music bound them together until it seemed that they were alone there, moving in perfect unison to an old familiar tune. Nothing else seemed to matter and for Ruth time itself seemed arrested. Tall and straight, Mark guided her expertly through the throng of dancers until, suddenly, the music ceased. It was time to go home.

Mark put his hand firmly under her elbow.

"I'll see you to your car," he said.

"I must collect Becky," she told him. "Ah, there she is!"

Becky came up to them, a half-nervous smile playing about her mouth. "Have you enjoyed yourselves?" she asked, not really looking at Mark.

"Very much," he answered, turning back to Ruth. "What's the programme for tomorrow?"

"Today, you mean." She smiled up at him. "Getting the sheep ready for the shearing, I expect. Work on a farm never stands still."

"We'd better go," Becky said with some urgency. "We could be holding up some of the other cars."

"Yes." Ruth was reluctant to leave. She wanted the evening to begin all over again; she wanted to feel Mark's arms about her, strong and reassuring, as his body was pressed against her own; she wanted to drift with the sound of music until there was no other sound but her own heartbeats thudding in her ears.

Yet, it really was over. They were back to reality and Mark was helping Emma Falconer on with her coat.

"What's the matter with you?" Becky demanded as they approached Lovesome Hill. "You've hardly spoken a word since we left Derham. Didn't you enjoy yourself, as you only danced with Mark Bradley once?"

Ruth pulled up in the courtyard before she answered. "Of course I enjoyed myself," she answered quietly. "That's what dances are all about."

"Mark's mad at Tim for letting me ride the yearling," Becky announced surprisingly. "He wants to see Tim in the morning. He wouldn't bawl him out at the Metcalfs'. Not the done thing to create a scene, I suppose."

Ruth was too tired to argue. Of course, Mark wouldn't create a scene. He wasn't made like that. He would deal with Tim at High Parks, perhaps dismiss him and maybe end his career, but he would do it quietly, giving no quarter if Tim continued to prove defiant. And Becky was partly to blame, she acknowledged, because she desperately wanted a horse to ride. Any horse.

Chapter Three

They awoke the following morning to a loud bleating of sheep, a discordant sound which cancelled out any pleasant dreams they may have had, to replace them with action.

"We've overslept," Ruth said as Becky ran downstairs in her wake. "Amos must be over at the pens or the ewes wouldn't be making such a noise."

"Amos is far too old," Becky objected. "We ought to have one of the gangs in to do our shearing like everybody else."

"We couldn't afford it," Ruth reminded her. "Amos will have to do."

"It's years since you did any shearing," Becky pointed out. "The first ewe you tackle will have you over on your backside in less than a minute."

"I'll have to take my chance." Ruth buttered some toast. "You'll be rolling and packing, by the way. Any objections?"

"Dozens." Becky examined her fingernails. "It's not the sort of work I like."

"Needs must," Ruth pointed out. "Leave the washing-up till we get back."

"If we ever do," Becky grumbled. "I know where I'd rather be."

"Back in York at your nice, cosy hostel," Ruth suggested. "Never mind. The exercise will do you good."

Two happy sheep-dogs bounded by their side as they walked to the pens where Amos was already working.

"Morning, Amos!" Becky called. "How's your back?"

"Better for seein' somebody to lend me a hand," the old shepherd assured her. "Farms don't run on their own."

Lovesome Hill was a two-hundred-and-twenty acre spread with a flock of six hundred sheep grazing on moorland, most of them already penned in the out field behind the barn which Ruth had prepared for their present task. It was difficult to talk with all the noise from the pens and the barking of the dogs who were in their element and she signalled that they were ready to start. It would take them all of six days to complete the task at one hundred ewes a day and she doubted if Amos could stay the course.

Pushing up her sleeves, she grappled with the first ewe, pulling it over on its side while she reached for the electric clippers.

"Tuck head in tha' legs," Amos advised her. "Does tha' no' remember?"

"I remember, Amos," Ruth gasped. "It's just getting the hang of it again after being away for so long."

"Tha'll learn," Amos grunted back. "Happen we'll manage fine."

A hundred sheep a day was more than Ruth cared to think about, but when she had passed her third fleece over to Becky to roll on the stretch of carpet she had spread on the scrubbed barn floor she felt a sense of achievement which she hadn't expected. It was hard work, but it left her strangely exhilarated. Becky tired long before she did.

"I'm covered in loose wool!" she complained. "Isn't it time for a break?"

"At eleven o'clock," Ruth told her relentlessly.

She was working near the door, in a shaft of sunlight, liberating the shorn ewes back into the open into the care

82

of Silver and Wraith who knew what to do with them, when the full light was suddenly cut off and a man's shadow stood between her and the noisy outside world. For a moment she was not quite sure who it was and then she knew that it was Mark.

She stood looking at him in utter surprise, unable to believe that he was really there.

"What have you come for?" she asked, fearing that it was Becky he had come to see.

"I thought you might need some help."

She saw that he was dressed for the task he wanted to share with her. The sleeves of his shirt were rolled to the elbow and he wore practical denim jeans thrust into fine kid boots which were laced almost to the knee. It was footwear she hadn't seen before – anyway, not in a Yorkshire Dale – and she stood staring at it for a further moment before he explained.

"I thought you might be working outside," he said, acknowledging Becky where she stood in the background with a perfunctory nod. "Where do you want me to start?"

Ruth gathered her thoughts together. "But you don't have to do this," she protested, the colour rising in her cheeks. "We could have managed—"

"Independence will get you nowhere," he said. "Have you an extra pair of shears?"

Ruth passed him her own clippers.

"Have you done this before?" she asked breathlessly.

"Hundreds of times," he assured her. "In Australia."

Her eyes opened wide. "I didn't know," she told him. "I thought you came from the other side of the Pennines."

"Originally," he admitted, "until I decided to chance my luck Down Under where I thought I'd get a better deal."

"And did you?" she asked, wanting to know more

83

about this strange man who had come to her rescue for the second time in so many weeks.

Mark shrugged. "I've never been sure about deals," he said. "They may look better from a distance – the grass always seeming greener on the other side of the fence – but you have to try them to make sure." He gazed into the distance where the sharp keel of the Pennines stood out against a cloudless sky. "I thought Australia was what I really wanted, but in the end I had to come home."

It was so like their experience with Jonathan that Ruth could not answer him immediately. Becky had disappeared with a murmured excuse and they were alone in the shed, with only the sound of the bleating sheep to isolate them, and it seemed that they were in a world apart.

"I don't really know very much about you," she said, "but I do thank you for coming to help. Believe me, I am grateful."

He smiled for the first time, the old amusement back in his eyes. "Which is a beginning," he acknowledged.

They worked side by side in comparative silence for over an hour, his pile of fleece dwarfing hers as he sent ewe after ewe back to the freedom of the fields where the two collies were waiting to round them up.

"You're shaming me!" Ruth confessed, pausing to relieve the pain in her back. "You work so fast."

"Habit," he said.

"And you don't like to be beaten by a woman," she suggested.

He straightened in his turn to consider her. "What do you want me to say?" he challenged. "That it depends on the woman? No, Ruth, I'm not the flattering kind," he added sharply. "I believe in calling a spade a spade."

"How Australian!" she laughed. "But you're not really an Aussie," she amended. "You're Yorkshire through and through."

"Tell me what you mean by that." He came to stand beside her. "I've a feeling it wasn't meant as a compliment."

She considered him in her turn. "Straightforward, blunt, never willing to take 'No' for an answer," she decided. "You've proved that already, but who am I to judge? You'll never alter."

A look that might have been pain passed across his eyes. "No doubt you're right," he said harshly. "It's all a matter of experience. We take the bull by the horns and go our own way, making our own mistakes, and when it's all over we have to come to terms with what we have left."

"Is – that what you are trying to do at High Parks?" she asked. "Coming to terms with disappointment, perhaps?"

"More or less," he conceded abruptly. "Since you ask."

She had angered him and she was immediately sorry. "I had no right to pry," she admitted awkwardly. "Anyway, it's time to take a break. There's coffee and something to eat up at the house."

She called to Amos as they left the barn and the three of them walked across the paddock to the kitchen door. Her mother was there waiting with the coffee pot percolating on the Aga, glad to see them.

"I watched you working with the girls in the barn," Hester told Mark. "We can't thank you enough for your help."

He waved her gratitude aside. "Call it being neighbourly," he said. "You'd do the same for me if the occasion arose."

Becky was hovering in the background, buttering scones.

"Are you coming back tomorrow?" she asked as they returned to the barn.

"I'm waiting to be asked," he countered with a sideways glance in Ruth's direction.

"Oh, my sister's too proud to ask," Becky informed him. "She's used to doing everything for herself."

"Becky, don't exaggerate!" Ruth said. "Pay no attention to her, Mark," she added hastily.

They worked side by side for another two hours while Amos fed them sheep from the pens and further conversation was stifled by the bleating of the ewes. It wasn't an easy job, but Ruth made few mistakes, falling into an old routine which she had previously enjoyed.

"My father taught me all I know," she informed Mark when they straightened their backs for a short rest. "This was always our busiest time of the year and we all took part – my brother Jonathan, Becky and me," she added for his enlightenment.

"My brother left home before my father died." Ruth was sorry she had spoken. "He went abroad – to Australia, as a matter of fact – and now we don't know where he is. We only have to hope that nothing has happened to him in the meantime."

"Where abouts in Australia?" Mark asked.

Ruth drew in a swift breath. "We last heard of him in Melbourne," she said, "but that was three years ago. He wanted to spread his wings, to see something of the world before he settled down. He was twenty-two."

"A vulnerable age." Mark picked up his clippers. "We all crave freedom in our own particular way. Why did you come home, Ruth?"

"Because I was needed." There was no hesitation about her reply. "I don't regret it. Not one little bit."

"Not even when you remember London and the kind of life you lived there?" he queried.

"Especially when I remember London!" Ruth smiled, following his gaze to the distant, rounded hills.

They ate their lunch at the kitchen door, sitting on the broad step in the sunshine while Hester passed cold ham and pickles out to them accompanied by hunks of home-baked bread which they consumed ravenously. Becky still continued to hover in the background, not too sure of Mark's reaction to her friendship with one of his grooms.

By the end of the day they had sheared more than a hundred sheep.

"You'll sleep well tonight," Mark said, getting back into his Land Rover. "See you tomorrow!"

"If you're sure." Ruth stood beside the open door of the vehicle, looking up at him. "You must have so much more to do."

"Nothing that can't wait," he assured her. "See you at first light!"

"Oh, hang on a minute!" she protested. "I have to sleep!"

"You will," he said. "As sound as a baby."

When he drove away she lingered in the barn thinking about him. He was an enigma to her and she might never come to understand him, but she knew that she liked him because he would never go back on his word.

It was a week before the remainder of the ewes were shorn of their woolly coats and returned to the freedom of the hills, a week in which Mark appeared regularly at eight o'clock each morning, not leaving till the light was beginning to fade. It made him almost one of the family, eating with them by mutual consent and doing more than half the work because he was so quick and efficient at the job. When Becky's enthusiasm flagged, as it did periodically, he thought of something else for her to do while he did the rolling and packing himself, untiring, it seemed, in his efforts to complete the week's work in record time.

Hester was loud in her praise of him. "He's a man after my own heart," she said. "Tolerant and fair, although I'm thinking he might not suffer disobedience gladly. He must be neglecting his own affairs up there at High Parks to come here, day after day, to lend us a helping hand."

Ruth had thought about that, but she had not attempted to thank Mark too often after he had swept her gratitude aside.

On the final day of the shearing she stacked the last fleece with an odd feeling of regret. It was all over now, their friendship and near intimacy, and she had little proof that it would be renewed as she watched Silver and Wraith usher the last shorn ewe back to the fold. Becky gathered up a coil of binding twine, flinging it on top of the stacked wool.

"'There will never be another you'," she sang joyfully. "There will never be another ewe – not for me, anyway!"

Mark followed her relieved progress back to the house with a whimsical smile. "She's irrepressible," he observed. "There will never be another Becky, I guess!"

"You've spoken to her about riding your horses?" Ruth asked.

"Not directly." A smile curved his lips. "I've warned Spurrier and given him a second chance."

"He'd be mad if he didn't take it," Ruth decided.

"I don't think mad is the right word. Irresponsible would fit the bill much better," Mark said. "Let's hope he'll take a telling."

"You've been more than generous," Ruth declared.

He shrugged, pushing his hat to the back of his head. "That remains to be seen." He took a swig from the bottle of home-made lemonade which had always been at hand while they worked. "I'll get back," he said. "Thanks for all the food – and the company."

It was over, Ruth thought once more, that long, sun-filled week when they had worked together in absolute harmony while the hours had passed so swiftly. Tentatively she put a hand on his arm.

"Thank you, Mark," she said. "Thank you for everything."

Suddenly she reached up to place a light kiss on his sun-warmed cheek and instantly she was in his arms. His mouth came down on hers in a hard, demanding kiss as her senses swam at his touch and her legs threatened to give way under her. The light in the shed dimmed, giving way before a hazy unreality as she clung to his hard body, feeling his strength and the warm closeness of him. An eternity seemed to pass before he released her, thrusting her from him so that she stumbled against the pile of shorn fleece Becky had left behind her so eagerly.

"Never do that again," he said harshly. "I don't need your gratitude, Ruth, or your cold little 'thank you' kisses."

She gazed up at him, unable to believe what she had just heard until pride rushed swiftly to her rescue, a pride which seared her heart even as she acknowledged it. "I won't ask you up to the house," she said coldly, "although I'm sure my mother will want to thank you, too. Good-night, Mark. If you ever need our help you have only to ask."

He bent to pick up his jacket, slinging it over his shoulders as he watched her go.

Hester came through to the kitchen as Ruth reached the open door.

"Was that Mark driving away?" she asked. "I thought he would be staying for a meal after all he's done for us this past week."

"No." Ruth could hardly answer her. "He wanted to be away."

Hester looked at her, acutely aware that she was upset. "What have you been saying to him?" she asked.

"Nothing. Nothing at all!" Ruth declared. "I tried to thank him in the only way I could, but he didn't understand."

"Happen it was just a lovers' tiff," Hester suggested, putting a kettle on to boil. "They soon blow over."

"Mother! We're not lovers. Don't think about it – ever." Ruth put a hand up to her throat as if something there was threatening to strangle her. "Mark doesn't trust anyone. Not even me."

Hester, in her wisdom, said no more.

Now that the shearing was done they had to turn their hand to haymaking and it seemed to Ruth that their busy way of life was a god-send because she had little time to think. She did not see nor hear of Mark for over two weeks, telling herself that she had to accept the fact that he was too busy at High Parks even to give them a second thought.

The hay meadow was at its best when she went up to look it over one afternoon, showing a prodigious variety of grasses and wild flowers which she was reluctant to disturb. That they would grow again she was fully aware. Nature did that, renewing everything in the spring, but somehow another spring seemed very far away. Walking knee-deep in buttercups, she lifted her face to the distant hills which bound the horizon. It was country she loved and would never grow tired of, but today it seemed stern and wild.

Before she reached the boundary wall she was aware that she was no longer alone. Mark was standing waiting for her at the gate, his arms folded across the upper bar, his cap pulled down over his eyes to shield them from the westering sun.

"Are you starting to cut up here?" he asked, opening

the gate for her to walk through. "What sort of help have you got?"

It was as if they had never had any difference of opinion, Ruth thought, as if he had never held her close, kissing her with a passion which had finally dissolved in anger as he had thrust her from him with words she would never forget. "Never do that again," he had said. "I don't need your gratitude or your cold little 'thank you' kisses."

Now he was looking at her as if all that had never happened, as if they were no more than mere acquaintances standing there on the moor edge with the sun-bright meadow behind them and a cool wind in their faces.

"I've got Amos and Becky," she told him. "The same as we had at the shearing."

"Hardly enough," he said. "I'll send you a man down in the morning."

"You don't need to, Mark," she objected. "We can manage. It's not such an energetic job as shearing all those sheep."

"Granted," he agreed. "But I'll still send someone to help if I can't get down myself."

All the way back to Lovesome Hill her tell-tale heart hoped that he would come. Haymaking had always been the highlight of their childhood days when they had ridden back to the farm on the hay with the dogs barking at the wheels and the warm sunshine on their faces, making them feel on top of the world. Nowadays most of the work was done in the meadow itself, with a machine to bale and wrap the hay in black plastic which would keep the rain out till they could take it back to the barns to store for their winter needs. The balers were hired locally with each farmer taking his chance of a suitable day. If they were lucky tomorrow would be fine and bright, Ruth thought, and most of the work could be done in a day.

"Someone's coming down from High Parks to help out," she told Hester over their evening meal.

"Who?" Becky demanded. "Do you mean Mark?"

"No. It could be one of the grooms," Ruth said. "Mark didn't mention anyone specifically."

"It won't be Tim, that's for certain," Becky returned. "Mark has got it in for Tim although he has given him another chance. The funny thing is," she added, "Mark thinks I'm a good rider. He's said so more than once and that's bound to mean something coming from someone like Mark Bradley."

"I wouldn't let it go to your head," Hester advised. "He can't be encouraging you and you'll only be making a nuisance of yourself if you persist in going up to the gallops again."

"When have I got the chance?" Becky wondered aloud as she rose to clear away the plates.

To both their surprise Mark came himself to help with the hay. It turned out to be one of those days when a light, drying breeze blew down from the hills and the sun shone endlessly, making their work a delight. Mark drove one of the harvesters with consumate ease, pulling up only occasionally to refresh himself with Hester's home-made lemonade which Ruth dispensed from a large plastic jug which had originally contained milk.

By midday half the meadow was cut.

"Time to eat!"

Ruth had brought a large picnic hamper down from the farm, spreading its contents on a tartan rug so that they could sit in the shade.

All morning Becky had been unusually quiet, looking towards the road from time to time as if she expected someone she knew to appear, but the road into Derham was quiet on this lovely early summer day with only the odd motorist to distract their attention from their task. The sound of the harvester had cut out all other sounds, but now the quiet had returned.

They ate in silence until Ruth observed, "It must all have been quite different for you in Australia, Mark."

He passed his coffee mug over to be refilled. "Not a lot different," he said, "except that it would be January. Most of our work was with sheep, of course, but the odd homestead had a meadow or two."

"I like that word 'homestead'," Ruth mused. "It says so much more than farm when you come to think about it."

His eyes grew grave. "It goes back a long way," he said. "The first settlers were mostly Scots and maybe they brought the word with them."

"Were you happy out there?" Becky interposed, getting up from her bale of straw to close the picnic basket. "Was it all you expected when you first went out?"

Tactless Becky! Ruth thought, seeing the look in Mark's eyes which suggested that he had not been completely happy for a very long time.

"At first," he said, "it filled the bill. I was, I suppose, a restless teenager wanting to spread my wings before I finally settled down. Yes, you could say I was happy enough. I had my freedom in a new environment. It was several years before I realized that I should come back to England because I had never seen eye to eye with my father."

"Like Jonathan," Becky said. "We never speak about him now, but we all miss him." She lifted the basket, her alert gaze suddenly back on the road. "I'll pop this in the car," she said. "I was going for a walk, anyway."

Ruth moved out into the sunshine. Amos had gone to sleep in the shelter of a tree and presently Mark joined her, sitting down on the grass at her feet.

"This is where you belong, Ruth," he said, leaning back on his elbows to thrust out his long legs in a complete

93

display of indolence which really didn't suit him. "You're not at all like Becky."

"Or even you," she countered. "Do you still hope to find contentment somewhere else?"

He plucked a tall grass from the patch above his head, considering her question.

"I've no great choice," he said, "now that I've taken over the responsibility of the family business. My grandfather started the quarries over at Pendlby on the far side of the Pennines and when my father was taken ill I came home."

So, that's where the money came from, Ruth mused; two highly successful quarries she had only heard about on the far side of the ice-scalped hilltops they could see in the distance so clearly today that it seemed she could almost touch them.

"High Parks must be more or less a hobby as far as you're concerned," she suggested.

He shook his head. "It's my home now, and it's something I've always wanted to do."

"You've changed it completely."

He lay back in the grass, gazing at the sky. "Not completely," he said. "Why don't you come up and see for yourself?"

Taken by surprise, Ruth didn't know what to say. "I – it's a very busy time on a farm," she faltered. "You must know that."

"I wasn't suggesting today or even tomorrow," he said. "When the autumn comes you'll have plenty of time. Tell me about Jonathan," he added abruptly. "Why does Becky say you never discuss him?"

"Because – lately we haven't been able to. Because we know how much hurt he inflicted on my mother by going away and because, deep in her heart, she believes he is dead," Ruth confessed.

94

The moment of silence between them seemed to draw them closer together.

"He'll come back," Mark said with amazing confidence. "Have you never heard of the Prodigal Son? I was one myself and I can't say they killed the fatted calf on my return, but it did make a difference to my mother. Since then my father has died and my sister and her husband live at Pendlby with my mother in the family home."

Hence High Parks, Ruth mused. Mark was too independent a character not to want a place of his own. Then there was Emma Falconer. He had admitted to finding her a home at Winterside Grange, possibly because he wanted her to be near him. Inevitably she remembered the gossip about him having had a bad experience of love which he couldn't forget. It was purely gossip, she tried to assure herself, brought back by Becky from her contact with Tim Spurrier who had said it was common knowledge at High Parks.

But where was Becky? Ruth rose from her comfortable seat on the hay bale to look across the shorn meadow to the field gate leading onto the road. Becky was there, leaning expectantly on the top bar waiting for someone to pass by.

"We have so many plans for Becky," she told Mark on an odd impulse. "She's always been the brainy one of the family and we're very proud of her, though we try not to spoil her."

Mark got to his feet, considering her wayward sister from a distance. "She must be a handful occasionally," he suggested. "She's a good little rider."

"Don't encourage her by telling her that all the time!" Ruth snapped back. "We have other plans for Becky."

"So I understand," he said, his eyes narrowing as Becky climbed up onto the gate. "You want her to stay on at York and justify your pride."

"Not at all!" Ruth turned to look at him, her eyes stormy. "We only want the best for her – the best she can achieve."

"Academically," he suggested. "That might not be all she needs."

"Becky's young for her age."

Mark smiled at her sisterly assumption. "She's eighteen, I believe. Old enough to know what she really wants, I would say," he observed. "Of course, I have nothing to do with it."

"No," she agreed. "So please don't try to interfere. We can deal with Becky in our own way."

"I wonder," he said, turning back to the harvester.

Amos stirred himself from what he called his "forty winks", coming back from the shade of the trees.

"Where's Becky?" he asked.

Mark looked beyond Ruth towards the field gate where Becky had been sitting a few minutes ago, his mouth suddenly hardening as he saw the two riders who had stopped on the road outside the gate. They were two of the grooms from High Parks and one of them was Tim Spurrier. Becky was now on the far side of the gate, holding onto Tim's stirrup as he bent to talk to her. Mark's jaw tightened as a dark colour suffused his cheeks.

"They've no right to be here," he said grimly. "They should be up at the gallops this afternoon and Spurrier knows that. It's obvious he hasn't learned his lesson."

A quiver of apprehension ran through Ruth as she looked up at him. Mark, in anger, could be disconcerting even if his rage was directed at someone else.

"What will you do?" she asked.

"Deal with him in my own way," he said, narrowed grey eyes still on the threesome at the gate. "I probably won't see him till the morning."

Becky came bouncing back across the meadow, seemingly much happier than she had been during the morning, while Mark set the harvester in motion without speaking to her.

"He's over-reacting," Becky said as she followed Ruth across the meadow. "I don't see any harm in chatting to Tim when he's out with one of the stud horses. He's exercising the yearling, for goodness sake!"

"Apparently he should have been up at the gallops," Ruth said, not wanting to be too deeply involved, "but Mark will have his own way of dealing with the problem."

"The way he deals with everything else," Becky suggested. "High-handed and imperious. You said so yourself not so very long ago, so what's changed you? Have you fallen in love with the man? If so," she added when Ruth made no immediate reply, "I'm sorry for you because he can't see any further than Winterside Grange."

The obvious reference to Emma Falconer seared across Ruth's mind like a rapier thrust. "I'm not in love with Mark," she defended herself quietly. "I hardly know him."

That was only a half-truth, she told herself, because in the last hour they had seemed to come very close. Lying there on the grass at the edge of the meadow he had revealed much of his past to her and some of his reasons for coming home. His experience had been uncannily like Jonathan's, in a way, although she realized that he hadn't told her everything. There was the rumour that he had known an unhappy experience of love, although it could easily be nothing but a rumour. She remembered how she had laughed when Becky had first mentioned it, calling Tim Spurrier a gossip. It all seemed so long ago that surely it wasn't true.

"We haven't seen much of Emma since Kate's party," Becky observed, rolling the first of the hay from the baler. "Do you think she might have gone somewhere? On holiday, perhaps?"

"I don't know," Ruth said almost too sharply. "Why don't you ask Mark?"

They separated, each to her appointed task, and when the final bale of hay rolled off the machine they were both tired and hungry.

"Are you going to ask Mark up to the house for something to eat?" Becky asked. "It's the right thing to do, isn't it?"

"I'll ask," Ruth agreed. "Though I don't think he'll come."

Surprisingly Mark accepted her invitation, following them to Lovesome Hill in his Land Rover to the immediate delight of Hester who had prepared a handsome meal for them all.

Amos took his in the kitchen, explaining that a chair with his back to the Aga was the best place for his rheumatism.

"Leave him be," Hester advised. "He'll eat more comfortably where he is and sleep it off afterwards on the rocker. Then he'll trudge home to that damp old cottage of his and think he's had a perfect day."

The table in the dining-room had been set for four so her mother had obviously expected an extra guest, Ruth thought.

"You'll be ready for a wash, I'm sure," Hester said. "There's towels aplenty in the bathroom. Up you go and make yourself at home."

Mark smiled across the room at her. "You think of everything," he said.

Ruth remained in the dining-room till Mark had negotiated the stairs.

"I suppose we'd better change," Becky said. "Although I'm hungry enough to eat directly from the Aga."

"Not in this house!" her mother informed her. "I'm not suggesting you put on a ballgown, but a fresh skirt and jersey would be nice."

Whether she should dress for Mark's benefit Ruth wasn't sure, but half an hour later she descended the oak staircase in a favourite two-piece which the family had not yet seen.

"That's nice," Hester acknowledged. "You suit green."

"She's doing it for Mark's benefit," Becky suggested wickedly. "Where is he, anyway?"

"Through in the kitchen speaking to Amos." Hester regarded her daughters each in turn. "Will you call him, Ruth?" she asked.

It was a meal that Ruth, at least, was to remember for a long time. The oak-pannelled dining-room faced her mother's garden at the back of the house, its mullioned windows looking out on a stepped rockery above which a host of multi-coloured flowers grew in wild profusion. It had been planted by two generations of busy housewives who had other tasks to fulfil but who had managed the odd moment to bring colour and beauty to a strip of land which they had cherished as their own. No one else worked in the garden and Hester had carried on where her mother-in-law had laid down her trowel. Now, in early summer, it was a riot of flowers, the scent of stocks drifting in through the open windows mingling with the heady perfume of pinks and carnations while beyond them the rose garden lay, half in sun and half in shade, waiting in the background for them to walk there if they felt so inclined.

Ruth felt that Mark was enjoying himself. He ate heartily, complimenting Hester on her culinary skill although the meal was plain enough.

"Away with you!" she returned. "I'm sure you eat just as well every day."

"We manage," he said. "We eat mainly out of supermarket cartons at present because I've yet to employ a cook. You couldn't recommend anyone suitable?" he asked. "She – or he – wouldn't need to live in."

Hester was obviously shocked by his news. "You mean you've been fending for yourself up there all this time?" she demanded. "What on earth have you been thinking about leaving all these young lads to eat what they like?"

"The grooms are all right," Mark defended his arrangements. "Someone comes in to look after them at the stables and they make their own beds and that sort of thing. The horses are their main concern. As long as there's enough food and nuts for their mounts they'd as soon eat at one of the pubs in Derham."

"Ay, fish and chips!" Hester snorted. "That won't keep them fit for long. And it won't do for you, either," she advised. "The sooner you get someone to look after you up at the house, the better."

"Oh, Mother, don't try your hand at matchmaking!" Becky laughed. "Mark's not the marrying kind."

"I'll have to look into that," Mark laughed in his turn, although Ruth felt that he was hardly amused. Becky had touched a raw spot, renewing a memory that had obviously hurt. She could have slapped her irresponsible young sister at that moment.

"We'll have to see about a housekeeper for you, even if she's only temporary at the moment." Ruth knew that her mother must have someone suitable in mind by the satisfaction in Hester's eyes. "There's a woman down Derham way I could recommend. I'll have a word with her."

Mark seemed reasonably satisfied. "She would only

need to come in for half a day," he decided. "Morning or afternoon to suit herself." He seemed indifferent to his own welfare. "I'm not there all the time. I go over to the quarries twice a week and I'm often in Ireland."

"Yet you'll help out a neighbour when you can," Hester pointed out. "We're grateful. You must know that."

Mark allowed himself a brief glance in Ruth's direction. "So I've been told," he said a trifle dryly. "Seriously, though, if you have any problems I'm more than willing to help out."

When he had gone Hester followed Ruth into the kitchen.

"He's paid his first half-yearly rent on the Pastures," she announced. "Brought the cheque with him this morning. It will make a difference, Ruth – a regular income which we're never really sure about these days. It's not a lot, but it will help pay Becky's way through university and maybe make it easier for us to have a bit of help in the house."

Ruth felt a slow colour rising in her cheeks. "I'm not complaining about the work I do, Mother," she said. "Surely you know that. It's being – dependent on someone else that rubs me up the wrong way, but I suppose that's foolish when Mark's only paying for something he wants."

"You don't like him," Hester suggested in evident surprise.

"I never said that." The colour deepened in Ruth's cheeks. "It was just the way he first went about try-ing to buy land we never wanted to sell that got my back up."

"Well, that's all sorted out now," Hester said. "Over and done with now that we've come to a bargain. I like the lad. He's honest and above board and I wouldn't like

101

any more friction to come between us. We're near enough neighbours to be friendly without living in each other's pockets, and that's always been our way in the Dales. Knowing Mark Bradley isn't going to change things, I'm sure."

It was also the way Mark wanted it, Ruth thought, as two weeks passed without any of them seeing him again.

"He's been in Ireland buying horses," Becky announced one morning after she had been to Derham to do some necessary shopping. "That's a dozen he'll have up at High Parks now. Enough to keep him busy for a while."

"How do you know about Ireland?" Ruth asked suspiciously.

"I – met someone." Becky looked beyond her. "No, not Tim Spurrier, if you have to know," she added. "It's all over Derham. Kate Metcalf told me."

Ruth drew in a swift breath of relief. At least Becky hadn't been pestering Tim Spurrier to ride one of Mark's horses in his absence.

"Can I keep your car for this afternoon?" Becky asked. "You won't be using it, will you?"

"No. I'm taking the dogs onto the hill," Ruth said, thinking about Mark.

If he had purchased more livestock in Ireland surely he meant to stay at High Parks for a very long time. It was typical of the man that he would have made his plans for the future very carefully and she could not help wondering what part Emma Falconer and her son, Harry, had in them. Emma, too, was a mystery, living over there at Winterside Grange on her own with only a small boy for company. She had been seen frequently by the locals, according to Amos, riding out with the pony on a lead because the boy

102

seemed nervous, but she had not returned to Lovesome Hill.

Perhaps that was asking too much of her, Ruth thought, although she had seemed reasonably friendly at the time. No doubt Mark spent much of his leisure hours at the Grange and was there more often than they thought.

When she called the two dogs she heard Becky laughing as she played with them around the barn, light, spontaneous laughter which seemed to echo right back to their childhood when they had run through the meadows together and frolicked in the sun. Those had been happy days, days to remember and bind them together for all time.

"I'll be back by six," Becky assured her. "Don't worry about the car!"

Ruth spent two hours on the moor, checking the flock with the two collies at her heels. The dogs were in their element, crouching low in the grass and bounding unexpectedly from the clumps of heather when a shorn ewe or an adventurous lamb wandered too far away. On the wide, open space of the moor there was a sense of freedom she hadn't known for a very long time as she breathed deeply of the fine, pure air. This was what belonging really meant. She never wanted to go away again.

Calling the dogs, she walked back to Lovesome Hill, taking her time because the sun was still high in the sky and there was no great urgency about her return. When she looked up at the farm it seemed to be steeped in peace, standing there against the hillside with the sun on its face and the shadows behind it. This was home, she thought; this was where she truly belonged. And Mark Bradley had made it a little easier for them to live there and keep Becky at university.

Thinking about him again, she approached the house

to hear the telephone ringing. Why was it, she wondered, that there always seemed to be an urgency about a ringing telephone bell?

"I'll get it!" she called to Hester who was in the sitting-room. "It could be someone for me."

"Lovesome Hill," she announced when she had lifted the receiver.

A man's deep voice she did not recognize spoke from the other end of the line. "Mrs Kendal?" it asked, going on before Ruth could correct the assumption, "This is the police. There's been an accident. I'm afraid your daughter has been seriously injured."

"Becky?" Ruth hardly recognized her own voice. "How? Where?"

"She has fallen from a horse she was exercising up at the gallops."

"Where is she?" Ruth gasped. "Where is she now?"

"She was taken to High Parks because it was nearest, but I'd say it was a case for the hospital. The doctor is up there now."

"I'll go there." Ruth let out a long, agonized breath. "I'll go up there right away."

Replacing the receiver, she was aware of a stunned, unbelieving silence in which the old grandfather clock in the corner of the hall ticked so loudly that it effectively obliterated all other sound. Her rigid body seemed glued to the spot, refusing to obey her demands on it, while her thoughts thundered out the enormity of the situation. It couldn't be true. This was a nightmare; this was something which should not be allowed to happen! Her mother had suffered enough.

"Who was that?" Hester asked from the comfort of the sitting-room.

"The police." Ruth was unable to lie to her even as she sought to protect her.

104

"What did they want?" Hester had come to the sitting-room door. "What's happened?" she asked when she saw her daughter's ashen face. "Has there been – an accident?"

"Yes," Ruth said tonelessly. "It's Becky. She's fallen from a horse."

For a moment Hester seemed incapable of answering her as sudden shock took over and then she said in a quiet, determined voice, her hand already reaching for her coat which hung behind them in the hall, "We must get there somehow, Ruth. We have to be with her right away."

"Yes," Ruth agreed, wondering how that was going to happen since they had no transport at their disposal. Becky had driven her car off to Derham in high spirits only a few short hours ago and now she was up there at High Parks, which was four miles away. "You can't walk. That's out of the question," she added, looking at her distressed parent. "I'll have to go alone."

Hester shook her head. "Somehow I've got to get there," she said.

Almost before she had uttered her desperate challenge the sound of a car's engine filtered through to them and a battered old Vauxhall turned in at the gate.

"It's the vet!" Ruth cried in unbelievable relief. "It's Chay!"

Chay Oliver pulled up at the end of the gravelled drive, his ruddy countenance pale with anxiety.

"I heard," he said, opening the back door of the car, "and I thought you might not have transport."

"Oh, Chay!" Ruth caught him by both hands. "I've never been so glad to see anyone in all my life."

"Hop in!" he said. "I'll get you up there in minutes."

Minutes that seemed more like hours. Ruth sat in the back seat beside her mother, holding one of her icy hands. Hester hadn't spoken since Chay's timely arrival and it seemed that the relief was too much for her. Sitting bolt upright in the back of the Vauxhall, one hand clutching her sturdy walking-stick, she kept her eyes steadily on the road ahead of them until they came to the entrance to High Parks.

"Those Stone Birds," she said at last. "They should never have been put back there. Mark should have left them where they were in the ditch."

Chay said, "They don't matter", or something to that effect, which did not register too clearly in Ruth's mind. All she wanted was to get to the house and clasp Becky in her arms as she had so often done when a younger Becky had cried after a distressing dream. But this was no dream. This was terrible, heartrending reality and her fingers tightened on her mother's hand as if to offer her further protection.

They swept round the curving drive to the front entrance of the house. High Parks stood some distance from the open-ended square of the busy stables, a stout Regency mansion with its face turned to the west and its many windows reflecting the glory of the dying sun. It looked deserted until they saw the two cars parked towards the rear of the building.

"They must have gone in by the side door," Chay decided, but before he could reverse the Vauxhall some-one had opened the main door and Mark hurried down the three shallow steps to meet them.

"I was about to send for you," he said, helping Hester out and leading her towards the steps. "Dr Bainbridge is with Becky. You can go straight in."

When he turned to face Ruth she had got out of the car and was standing beside Chay, still too shocked to put her feelings into words.

"I'm sorry about this," he said. "You'll want to see her right away."

106

"Of course I want to see her." Ruth's voice was no more than a whisper. "We're family. You ought to understand that."

He saw her distress, leading her without more ado to where her mother was waiting in the vast unfurnished hall. Before them what seemed to be an endless staircase spiralled upwards leading, it seemed, to nowhere.

"She's in here," Mark said, indicating a massive door which stood partly open, letting out a pale gleam of sunlight.

He took Hester by the arm, leading her gently forward. Ruth could see the broad curve of his powerful shoulders and the line of dark hair growing low on the nape of his neck and suddenly everything seemed to be concentrated on that one glimpse of him as he stood aside to let her pass.

The room they entered was still bright, although heavy curtains had been drawn at one end of it to shield Becky's face from the sun. Ruth held her breath. Her sister was lying spread-eagled on a *chaise-longue* like a rag doll flung down by a petulent child, her blonde hair flowing back from her head like some sort of cloak to protect her. Hester dropped her stick and knelt down beside her wayward child.

"We're here, Becky," she said. "We're here!"

The doctor motioned Ruth aside, his lined, weather-beaten face grave with concern.

"We've done all we can for her at the moment," he said. "We can't do more. I've sent for an ambulance. It will be here in under an hour."

An hour, Ruth thought. Surely they could do better than that! She turned to the doctor who had brought her into the world twenty-four years ago.

"Don't break this to my mother," she begged. "You can tell me the worst."

George Bainbridge led her to one of the windows. "She's injured the base of her spine," he explained. "It's serious, Ruth. She may never walk again."

The stark, terrible truth hit Ruth like a bombshell. Becky might never walk again, glorious, golden Becky, who had taken life and love and laughter in her stride, might be confined to the shadows for the rest of her life. She could not – would not believe it. Some heartless quirk of fate had decreed this, but they must fight it with all their combined wills!

She saw her mother in deepest distress kneeling by the *chaise-longue*, felt the tears she could not shed burning behind her own eyelids while absolute helplessness gripped her by the throat. How could this have happened, she wondered, to Becky of all people?

"You're shaken," George Bainbridge said. "It's been a nasty shock for us all, although we did wonder about Bradley allowing her to ride such a spirited horse, especially up there on the Pastures."

Ruth stared at him. "Mark," she said. "Was Mark there when it happened?"

"He couldn't have been too far away," the doctor decided. "He brought her back here. It was the nearest place without moving her too much. In that he was sensible."

The words drifted above Ruth's head. Mark had been up there at the gallops, Mark, who had encouraged Becky by telling her that she was a good little rider all those weeks ago. If anyone was to blame it was Mark!

She didn't really believe that, she tried to convince herself. He had acted swiftly and decisively in an emergency which was what she would have expected of him. He had brought Becky here and sent for the doctor and an ambulance and he may even have saved her life. When she thought of Becky dead she found herself shaking from head to foot.

Turning back to the *chaise-longue* she stood beside her mother, waiting for Becky to speak.

"Keep talking to her," George Bainbridge encouraged them. "Keep her mind alert."

Becky opened her eyes once. For a fleeting moment her brilliant blue gaze focused on Hester's face before the long lashes fluttered and closed again. Becky gave a small sigh which sounded like relief.

Ruth turned away. Would the ambulance never come? She stood at the window overlooking the drive, waiting, waiting.

After what seemed an eternity Mark came into the room, his face frozen in anxiety. "You'll want to go with her," he said.

Ruth gazed back at him, her heart in turmoil. "Of course," she said tonelessly.

He did not offer her his sympathy. How could he, Ruth wondered, if he was solely to blame?

Someone in the outer hall called, "They're here!" and she heard the crunch of wheels on gravel through the open doorway. After that everything seemed a terrible blur: two men carrying a stretcher and another in a white coat bending over her defenceless sister. Then they were carrying Becky out wrapped in a red blanket with only her pale, rigid face showing to say who she was.

Ruth turned back to her mother, retrieving Hester's walking-stick from the polished wood floor where she had been kneeling with her daughter's listless hand in hers for the past half-hour.

"We're going with her," she said. "Chay will take us."

It was Mark, however, who finally drove them to the hospital in the wake of the ambulance.

"I'll go down to Lovesome Hill," Chay offered, "and help Amos with the stock. After that I'll follow you to the hospital."

He must have wanted to go with Becky all the way, Ruth thought, but he was offering a needed service instead which would keep her mother from worrying about the farm. They were all in this together – all of them. Even Mark.

She sat in the back of his car with her arm about her mother's shoulders while Hester sat beside her, frozen in silence, a continuing prayer on her lips.

When they finally reached the hospital they were shown into a small side ward where the endless waiting began. Becky had been whisked away out of their hands into the tender care of nurses and doctors, x-rays were taken, people passed and re-passed outside the open door. A nurse came with cups of tea, trying to smile reassuringly even though she could not give them any real comfort. Ruth tried not to look at her mother too often, restraining herself from getting to her feet each time someone approached the door. Hester, in her own indomitable way, sat gazing at the wall in front of her, reading and re-reading a poster about health care in the home, all of which she already knew.

After what seemed an eternity an older man in a white coat came to speak to them. Closing the door behind him, he sat down beside Hester. "She's comfortable," he said, seeing beyond the steady resolve in her face to the turmoil within. "She's taken a nasty fall, Mrs Kendal, but we'll do everything we can for her. She's in no immediate danger, I can assure you, so I think you should go home and try to get a good night's sleep. Then, in the morning, you can see her again. Have you someone who can bring you down?"

Hester nodded. "We'll manage," she said, getting

reluctantly to her feet. "We'll manage fine. My daughter has a car."

For the first time since Becky's accident Ruth wondered about her car. Where had Becky left it in that mad rush to ride Mark's horse? Probably at the gallops, she decided, or further afield at the Pastures. Maybe if they hadn't allowed Mark that lease on the Pastures this would never have happened.

Tired as she was, the thought pursued her all the way back to Derham with Chay Oliver driving faster than usual because there was so much to do before nightfall. He had been waiting in the hospital car-park when they had emerged, looking for Mark, and he had only been able to ask about Becky, his ruddy face creased in dismay.

"I told Bradley not to wait," he explained, "and he seemed to have other things to do."

They took Hester straight back to Lovesome Hill.

"You see to your car," she directed Ruth. "I'll be all right."

Amos was there, attending to the pigs and closing in the hens.

"I'll wait till them gits back," he promised. "See to car!"

Chay drove Ruth to Derham and along the moor road to the Pastures where her car was sitting contentedly beside the tarn.

"I'll wait till you check," Chay offered.

The key was still in the ignition, which was careless of Becky, but Ruth heaved a sigh of relief.

"Thanks, Chay," she said. "Thanks for everything. Just you get home now. I'll manage."

She did not start the car immediately he had gone. Instead she sat staring into space, reviewing all the sad happenings of the past few hours. It was impossible to imagine life at Lovesome Hill without Becky or even with Becky in a wheelchair, and what all this would do to her mother was beyond contemplation. Hester had suffered enough.

She got out of the car again to feel the wind in her face, a cool evening wind blowing straight down from the hills, and it was several minutes before she realized that she was no longer alone. A man was coming towards her along the narrow moor road, a tall, broad-shouldered man with the purposeful stride she recognized immediately. It was Mark.

All the pain and anxiety of the long day seemed to crowd into that moment of recognition as she turned to face him. "Why are you here?" she asked automatically.

"I came to look for your car." He was close now, searching her face with those demanding grey-blue eyes. "I thought I could return it to Lovesome Hill."

"Then – you knew where Becky had left it." The words choked in Ruth's throat.

"I knew she was up here – yes," Mark said.

"Because you encouraged her." Her voice was cold with accusation. "You said she was a 'good little rider' and that meant to Becky that one day she could ride professionally." All the trauma of the long, sad day seemed to be concentrated in these last few words. "I'll never forgive you for this, Mark," she cried. "Never!"

His face darkened as he stepped nearer, catching her arm in a hard grip. "Never say never, Ruth," he said savagely. "It's too negative a word for someone like you, and when you come to regret it you'll find it twice as hard to reverse your decision."

"I'll never do that," she told him, struggling to free herself. "I'll always see you as you are."

Breathing deeply, she put her hands against his chest, conscious of the wild beating of her truant heart against

112

the hard insistence of his body as he continued to hold her.

"Why struggle?" he asked. "You have only to say the word and I'll let you go. I have no interest in holding you against your will. You must know that."

The cold indifference in his voice struck deeply, finding a vulnerable part of her which she sought to deny. "Let me go!" she cried. "I don't want to see you ever again."

"You don't mean that," he said as he released her. "Simply because you know it's unlikely when we live so close in a small community like Derham. We'll see each other, Ruth, time and time again, and you must make of it what you will. I'm quite indifferent."

Confused and angry, she turned towards her car. "You're – impossible," she told him. "No wonder you're alone up there in your special Ivory Tower at High Parks. You could never really mix, could you? You have to have everything your own way all the time. You have to be the arbiter of everyone's fate."

He bent to close the car door for her. "Learn to live with disappointment, Ruth," he said quietly. "Becky will go her own way. Surely you have recognized that before now."

"I know that I have almost lost a sister," she all but sobbed. "I know that Becky may never walk again as a free spirit up here among the hills. She's going to be crippled, Mark – perhaps crippled for life. How are we going to explain to her when most of her living is still before her? Can you tell me? Can you put it into words, for I can't. There is nothing I can think to say that will console her because it is something she will never be able to accept."

Bending closer, he put a comforting hand over hers. "Go home," he said. "Get back to your mother. She must need you."

The tone of his voice had changed completely. There

was pity in it and understanding, even compassion as she tried in vain to start the engine.

"Do you want me to drive you back?" he asked.

"No. No, I can manage."

"Not always, Ruth," he suggested. "Once in a while you must need help."

She turned the ignition key a second time and the engine roared into life.

"Thanks for coming," she said, forcing back the tears. "Thanks for thinking about the car."

"I had a fair idea where it would be," he said above the sound of the revving engine, "and I knew you would need it."

She reversed the car across the road, aware of him standing there watching until she was finally out of sight. Perhaps he did care about Becky more than she thought.

Chapter Four

It was several weeks before Becky came back to Lovesome Hill in a wheelchair, weeks in which they travelled backwards and forwards to the hospital with hope in their hearts and a prayer on their lips.

They had spoken little of the future as they had listened to the surgeon's verdict, realizing that it was now up to them to make Becky's life as happy as they could. It would be a long haul for all of them, and especially Becky. One day she might walk again, but there was no guarantee of that.

Faithfully Chay had visited the hospital week after week, making time from his busy and expanding practice to express his love in the only way he could. He filled Becky's side ward with flowers and chocolates and anything else that she could eat, holding her hand on occasion when she wanted to cry. When she was told that she could come home to the dale it was Chay she asked to bring her.

"You've got a car big enough to cope with this silly contraption I've acquired," she told him, gripping the arms of the wheelchair till her knuckles showed white, "and there's nobody else I can ask."

Chay was content with that, driving her back to Lovesome Hill on a bright September day when the distant ridge of the Pennines was hazy against the western sky and the narrow dale lay blissfully at peace.

Ruth and her mother had waited for this day with high hopes in their hearts, but to see Becky still in her wheel-chair was almost more than they could bear. Becky herself was putting on a brave face, allowing the two collies to lick her all over as they pranced around her chair, smiling when she saw the effort they had made to refurbish her father's old office on the ground floor to convert it into a temporary bedroom for her convenience. Ruth had even remembered to bring Mr Bruin down from her bedroom to sit perkily on her new bed, a gesture which Becky acknowledged by hugging the disreputable bear close as she looked around her at her new accommodation.

"You've been terribly busy," she said. "This'll do fine."

In all the weeks since her accident she had never mentioned Tim Spurrier's name. Nor did she refer to Mark.

Mark, Ruth thought, had passed completely out of their lives. Of course they had heard about him from time to time: he was in Ireland again; he had gone to London; he was spending days on the far side of the Pennines working at the Bradley Quarries with his brother-in-law whom they had never met.

Ruth thought about him constantly, knowing that she ought to apologize to him for her impassioned outburst that day up at the tarn, but how could she do that after what he had said? Some day she might be able to explain it all, but words were too difficult now. Besides, she never saw him.

A week after Becky's return they had an unexpected visitor. Emma Falconer rode up to Lovesome Hill on her fine horse, leading her small son on Becky's former pony. Becky saw them first from where she was sitting in her wheelchair in the sun watching the swallows swooping low over the barn rooftop. She had a little bell by her side to summon help if she needed it and she rang it loudly for Ruth's attention.

Emma had got down from the saddle by the time Ruth appeared at the open door.

"Hullo!" she said. "I hope you don't mind a visitor so early in the morning."

"It's well on in the day so far as we're concerned," Ruth assured her, going forward to shake her by the hand. "It's nice to see you – and Harry," she added, including the small, pale-faced child in her welcome.

"Harry wanted to bring Beauty to see Becky," Emma said. "He thought she might be anxious about him."

Ruth helped Harry down from the saddle, wondering how Becky would take this meeting with dear old Jet. He was a very sober little boy, small for his age and painfully thin, with large violet-coloured eyes like his mother's and Emma's pale, almost transparent complexion, which no amount of summer sun had managed to tan to a healthier hue.

Becky propelled her chair across the cobbles to be greeted with a whinney of delight by her old favourite.

"Jet!" she cried as the pony nuzzled her shoulder. "How are you, you old softie? I see you've put on far too much weight."

"We call him Beauty now," Harry advised her shyly. "Do you think that's a better name?"

"Much better," Becky agreed. "Apart from the weight he's looking very well."

"I brush him every day," Harry offered. "He's got his own brush and a curry comb just for himself – and his own blanket," he added for her further enlightenment.

"I've never heard him talk so much to a stranger," Emma smiled at Ruth as she looked affectionately at her son. "Mark is the only other person who can get him out of his shell."

"How is Mark?" Ruth asked, trying to keep her tone impersonal. "We haven't seen him for some time."

"He's such a busy person," Emma said. "At present he's back in Ireland buying bloodstock but he ought to be home at High Parks by the weekend. I keep telling him that he's doing far too much, rushing around from place to place all the time as if there were no tomorrow, but he doesn't listen. Men never do," she added with her rare smile. "They don't see the need for a middle course. It's all or nothing with them until they realize that they're missing out on something important."

"I don't think Mark will ever miss out on the important things," Ruth said stiltedly. "Will you stay for some coffee? My mother will be pleased to see you."

Why had she thrust her mother's name to the fore like that, she wondered, making it seem that only Hester would be pleased to accept their visitor? Perhaps that was because of Mark, too, because she could see Emma as his natural choice, a rich widow who could also be his friend. Hurt assailed her at the thought, although she had yet to convince herself that she was in love with Mark.

They drank their coffee on the raised terrace overlooking the dale, because it was still warm enough to sit outside and they could watch the tethered horses grazing contentedly in the paddock as they talked. Becky was evidently enchanted by young Harry who didn't seem to notice her disability, while Emma had quickly found a kindred soul in Hester who gladly showed her over her garden while Ruth carried the used crockery back to the kitchen to be washed up. She was scalding the coffee percolator when she realized that Emma was standing at her side.

"I had to come to ask about Becky," she said. "Mark is most concerned about her."

"We're on the telephone." Ruth could hardly keep the

118

bitterness out of her voice. "Our number wouldn't be too hard to find."

Emma took up a towel to dry the percolator. "He wasn't responsible, Ruth," she said quietly. "Mark didn't give Becky his permission to ride that horse."

"He encouraged her to think she could ride professionally."

Emma shook her head. "Mark wouldn't do that. Not until she had far more experience. It was one of the grooms who let her ride at the gallops. Tim Spurrier. He had a crush on Becky."

"Where is he now?" Ruth asked.

"Dismissed, of course," Emma said. "Mark had cautioned him twice before but he took no notice. I don't know where he is now. Probably somewhere in the south looking for another job."

It was impossible not to feel a sense of relief, Ruth admitted as she turned to look at Emma who was obviously Mark's confidante.

"I can't say I'm sorry," she confessed.

"Let's hope he won't come back," Emma said. "Becky can very well do without him. I remember seeing them at the Metcalfs' party and he seemed all wrong for her. The vet, now; he's a different story. He's such a nice man."

"He's been one of Becky's admirers for a very long time," Ruth said. "Let's hope – all this doesn't discourage him."

"It won't if he is truly in love with her," Emma decided quickly. "He'll run the course, you'll see."

"Even if Becky is never able to walk again?"

Emma took a moment to answer her before she said, almost defiantly, "Somehow I think she'll get out of that chair one of these days through sheer determination, because she's that sort of person. She won't accept defeat."

Ruth took the tea-towel from her, hooking it back onto its peg.

"I wish I had your confidence," she said. "We're all so terribly involved. My mother has had enough to bear – my brother's disappearance, my father's death, the shock of her illness, and now this."

"Mark told me about Jonathan," Emma said with evident sympathy. "That must be almost as bad as someone you love dying – not knowing where he is. Mark had a similar experience, you know. It was some time ago, but he knew he had to come back even before his father died. He owed it to the family, you see. It was a kind of debt as far as he was concerned."

She knew so much about Mark, Ruth thought, which suggested that they must have been friends – or lovers – for a very long time.

"He told me about his father," she said, moving towards the door. "It's funny how these things duplicate each other all the time. Jonathan like Mark, very determined to do his own thing."

"Like most of us!" Emma laughed. "But sometimes circumstances overwhelm us. We imagine ourselves in love and go off at a tangent and marry the most unsuitable person to our ultimate sorrow. I married very young and had Harry almost immediately. Then—" She paused for a moment, gazing out across the paddock where Becky and her son were inspecting the pony. "Then my husband died," she added under her breath. "A sad little story when you come to think about it," she said quietly.

I like her, Ruth thought. I want to like her because she is so beautiful and so truthful, so lacking in vanity and so obviously willing to be friends. If Mark and she were genuinely in love that shouldn't make any difference, but the difference it did make was a deepening of the hurt within her own heart.

"I'd like to come back," Emma said when she was in the saddle again. "I'd like to be able to call on you occasionally, if you really can't come to the Grange for a while."

"We're not calling folk," Hester told her with a rare smile, "but you'll be more than welcome here whenever you like to come."

When mother and son had rode off Hester turned to her elder daughter. "I like her," she said. "She's the sensible sort wi' few airs about her. It's a pity she was widowed so young. That little lad needs a father to help bring him up and maybe put some stamina into him. A woman was never meant to rear a family on her own."

"Some of them do very well," Ruth said teasingly. "Look at you, now! You're managing fine."

"Happen I was over-ambitious about Becky," Hester admitted with a sigh as she watched her younger daughter manipulating her wheelchair across the cobbled yard, "but you have to cope with an accident the best way you can." She looked back at Ruth with a far-away expression in her eyes. "There's only you now, Ruth," she said. "I'd like to see you happily married with a place of your own – and children."

Pointedly she hadn't mentioned her son's return. It was as if she had finally given up hope of Jonathan ever coming home again.

Becky had good days and bad days to contend with in the weeks that followed. There were days of cheerfulness as she careered in her wheelchair across the cobbles of the yard, challenging them all to find a suitable name for her new means of propulsion.

"What am I to call this?" she would ask, rattling the arms of the chair. "The Go-cart? No. The Buggy. Becky's Buggy! That's it! I need a big, painted sign to put across the back so that everyone will know."

There were other days when dark depression descended on her little world, sweeping the laughter from her lips and the merriment from her blue, blue eyes; days when she could see nothing ahead of her but disappointment and despair.

Ruth and Hester did what they could, thinking up little tasks for her about the house and garden that she could tackle easily enough, but finally it was Mark who made a difference. Unexpectedly he arrived at Lovesome Hill on a cold autumn morning when they were all indoors. He had two white doves with him in a wicker basket and a dove-cote to see them properly housed.

"I thought Becky would like to have these," he said. "My sister keeps them at the Quarry House and the children love them. They're gentle things and don't need much attention."

Ruth had opened the door to him, her heart beating strongly at this unexpected encounter. "Will you come in?" she asked. "Becky is just having her breakfast. She sleeps downstairs now in my father's old office."

She hadn't meant to emphasize the fact that Becky could no longer negotiate the stairs by herself, but Mark said humbly enough, "I'm sorry about all this, Ruth. Deeply sorry because it need not have happened."

"I know." She had no intention of accusing him again. "There's no point in apportioning blame. Not now."

"Yet you still consider me responsible." It was a statement rather than a question and she saw the gleam of anger in his eyes which was quickly repressed. "I thought we might have a word."

"About Becky?" she asked. "Mark, there's nothing you can say about Becky, nothing that will do any good. She has taken this reasonably well, but all the presents in the world won't make up for the loss of her freedom. I'm not blaming you. I don't hold you responsible any

122

more, but I think it would be better if you didn't come too often."

"Or not at all?" He set the dove-cote down on the cobbles. "I'd rather hear that from your mother – or Becky," he said.

"Oh, Mark!" Her heart was full of remorse. "I shouldn't have said that. It's just that I don't want Becky hurt any more. Seeing you might bring back all the agony of the past."

"Who's that?" Becky's young, high-pitched voice demanded from the hallway. "Who's there? Is it Chay?"

"No," Ruth answered. "It's Mark. He's brought you a present."

There was a long pause before Becky piloted herself across the hall towards them. She had been late up, but as usual she had dressed herself carefully, brushing out her hair to a blonde halo about her pale face. Becky had never needed make-up, Ruth thought, she was naturally lovely and today her fair skin seemed to glow.

"Hullo, Mark," she said with just a hint of diffidence. "Why don't you come in? Visitors are always welcome." Her keen gaze went beyond him to the dove-cote. "Especially visitors bearing gifts!" she added with a grin.

"Weren't you taught to beware of such people?" Mark challenged, returning her smile.

"Surely it applied only to the Greeks," Becky said. "Or maybe it was some other foreigner. Anyway, what's inside the dove-cote?"

"Doves, of course. I thought you might like to have them." He stood beside her chair looking down at her with infinite pity in his eyes because her attention was focused elsewhere. "They're breeding like rabbits over at the Quarry House."

Becky laughed outright. "I've never heard of flying

rabbits before," she declared. "Are you sure your sister wanted to part with them?"

"Danielle was only too eager," Mark assured her. "Especially when she knew they would be going to a good home."

"They'll look nice in Mother's garden," Becky said. "Above the rockery, I would say. Can I hold one?"

He took the wicker basket from the back of his car, producing a pure white dove for her to hold and Becky took it from him, pressing it gently against her cheek.

"This is good of you, Mark," she said huskily. "What shall I call them?"

"Romeo and Juliet springs to mind," Mark suggested.

"You're not very original, are you?" Becky held out her hand for the second dove. "Of course, they *are* the original love-birds, aren't they? Have you got a pair at High Parks?"

Mark looked surprised at her question. "They're not exactly my cup of tea," he told her. "Besides, we're not as sheltered up there as you are here."

"That's true," Becky agreed. "I'll get Amos to fix the dove-cote for me right away."

Mark looked round to where Ruth was standing beside the kitchen door. "Do you approve?" he asked. "It was something I thought I might do for Becky."

"Why do you think I would disapprove?" she asked, quick tears welling behind her eyes. "It was a lovely thought, Mark, and Becky is certainly grateful."

"I'd like to come again," he said bluntly. "Unless you object."

"Why should I?" The tears were nearer than she thought. "I can't forbid you to come."

His jaw tightened a fraction. "That makes a difference," he said.

124

"You'll stay?" she invited.

"Since you insist. I've also come to have a word with your mother about the Pastures."

Ruth bridled immediately. "I hope you're not going to upset her or try to persuade her to do anything against her will," she said.

"No. A bargain is a bargain." He turned to help Amos with the dove-cote. "It's just a question of fencing in that section of the moor. I would have to have her permission to go ahead with it. I'd pay, of course. For the fencing," he added briefly.

"I don't think she will stand in your way," Ruth said, "but you'll have to ask."

He followed Amos round the gable end of the house while Becky propelled herself after them with the wicker basket containing the love-birds on her knees.

"What brought Mark Bradley to the door so early in the morning?" Hester wanted to know, coming through to the kitchen where Ruth was busy with the coffee percolator. "Did he want something?"

"He brought Becky a present," Ruth said without turning round, "and he also wanted to see you."

"What about?" Hester asked sharply.

"Fencing in the moor end of the Pastures."

"I couldn't afford that," Hester declared. "Fencing is a terrible price these days. It would nearly be cheaper to build a dry-stone wall."

"Mark doesn't expect you to pay for the fence," Ruth told her. "He's quite willing to do it himself, only he needs your permission."

"That's reasonable enough," Hester acknowledged. "What had he got in the back of his car?"

"A dove-cote."

"A – what?"

"A dove-cote and two white doves. They're something

125

to take up Becky's attention when it's too cold for her to sit outside."

"By way of appeasement?"

Ruth considered the suggestion. "I don't think so. I don't think Mark would – stoop to that sort of thing. He genuinely wants to help."

"Does that mean you've changed your mind about him?"

Her mother's question was so unexpected that Ruth dropped the percolator lid. "I think I have," she said slowly. "I don't think he was at all to blame for Becky's accident."

"Then why don't you tell him so?" Hester demanded. "He deserves that if you accused him in the first place."

"I know." Ruth swallowed hard. "But somehow I don't think he would accept an apology after what I said."

"You could try him," Hester suggested. "Maybe he's not as proud as you think."

When Becky returned she could talk of nothing but the doves. "You should see how they cuddle up to one another," she told Ruth. "It doesn't take much imagination to know they are in love."

"You'll come through to the sitting-room and we can talk," Hester suggested and Mark followed her obediently.

"He's never said one word about that horse," Becky marvelled when they had gone. "It was a terrible thing for me to do, I suppose, but he doesn't blame me. What he was really angry about was the way Tim defied him after being warned. Tim knew he was doing wrong." There was a pause in which Becky seemed to review the situation in a much clearer light. "I suppose I used Tim for my own ends, but I desperately wanted to ride and Mark's horse was better than none." She twined nervous fingers in her long, curling hair. "I was a silly fool, Ruth. Nobody could call me anything else. I've always had what I wanted and this is the result." She looked down at her useless legs. "But one day I'll walk again. I know I will! However long it takes I'm going to best this and Mark is going to help. He knows I'll need all the support I can get."

"Becky," Ruth said gently, "we're all behind you in this. I'd give anything – just *anything* to see you well and happy once more."

"I know you would," Becky said, clasping her by the hand. "You're the sacrificing kind. You were always giving me things when we were kids – that doll's pram you valued so much and your first pair of skis. We don't have so much snow as we did in those days," she remembered. "The dale used to be full of snow and the moor was covered in it for weeks. Don't you remember?"

"I remember you falling down a pot hole when you were only seven," Ruth agreed. "We thought we had lost you, when you popped up as bright as a button at the other side."

"That was at the Caverns," Becky mused. "I was really scared that time, but I guess I am a survivor." She gazed through the open window to the ridge of the hills above Winterside. "I'll overcome this, too, Ruth," she said. "Just see if I don't!"

When Hester and Mark rejoined them they both looked satisfied.

"I'll start on the fencing right away," Mark promised. "Don't worry about it." He looked past Hester as if to include Ruth in his assurance. "Best to get it out of the way before the winter sets in."

"You haven't experienced a winter in the Dales yet," Hester reminded him. "They can be tough."

"I've a good idea," he told her, "and in some ways I'm looking forward to it."

"We can be snowed up for days on end," Becky warned. "You might not be able to get away if the dale road is closed."

"I've even made provision for that – plenty of fodder and extra bedding for the stables and food enough for me," Mark explained.

Which meant that he intended to make High Parks his permanent home, Ruth thought, feeling curiously relieved, although why it should concern her personally was quite another matter.

Drinking their coffee in the companionable warmth of the kitchen it seemed that he was no longer a stranger, the new owner of High Parks who seemed determined to live an isolated existence up there at the stud without becoming too much involved in the life of the dale. Hester liked him; there could be little doubt about that since she obviously trusted him to fulfil his part of any bargain they might strike, and Becky was suitably impressed.

"I started out thinking he was some kind of ogre," she confessed to Ruth when Mark had finally departed, "but he's been absolutely magnanimous about the horse episode. He's just sort of brushed it aside as something that shouldn't have happened and won't happen again. You've got to like him, Ruth whatever you think about him not belonging."

"Did I say that?" Ruth asked. "I'm sure I never thought it. High Parks has always been part of the dale and when the Jeffs had it we were friendly enough."

"I wonder where they went," Becky mused. "After the old man died."

"Canada, I think." Ruth gazed out of the window. "They lost a lot of money, I believe, and High Parks has taken a long time to sell."

"Well, it's back to normal now and thriving," Becky said. "I guess Mark will marry one day and fill it with children as it was meant to be. Surely he must have someone in mind?"

Ruth's thoughts flew to Emma Falconer, who must surely be Mark's ultimate choice. Tall and sophisticated, Emma would grace High Parks with her presence, making Mark a suitable wife. They had known each other for a long time, apparently, and seemed to have much in common.

"Did you know Mark was Harry's godfather?" Becky asked as if she had anticipated Ruth's thoughts. "Tim told me. He said Mark was crazy about him and must be keen on his mother as well. The last bit was stable gossip, of course, but Tim said the bit about Harry was true. Maybe that's why Mark goes so often to the Grange. Maybe that's why he bought dear old Jet for Harry to ride."

The fact that the pony was no longer her prized possession did not seem to upset her now, but Ruth was amazed to hear her talking about Tim Spurrier so casually. If she had put him completely out of her life that was an advantage, of course, but somehow Ruth could not be absolutely sure.

Becky's life and, indeed, her own was full enough at present. Two days a week there was the long and tiring journey to Out Patients at the hospital for an exhausting session of physiotherapy which was considered essential for Becky's partial recovery and this had to be sandwiched in between Ruth's other household chores. It had been a relief, therefore, when Chay Oliver had offered his help, whisking Becky and her chair away for a whole morning in his roomy old Vauxhall, and sometimes not returning with her till late in the afternoon. Emma had come to Ruth's rescue once or twice, driving up in her spacious family car to take Becky to the hospital appointment and then to lunch at an hotel on the way back.

The simple pattern of their lives seemed to resolve

around Becky and Ruth was not too greatly surprised when Mark also offered his help. He drove down to Lovesome Hill early one morning while Ruth was preparing to leave.

"I'm going to Harrogate," he explained. "I thought I might drop Becky at the hospital on my way and save you a journey. I could pick her up again when she's had her treatment. Ruth," he added when he thought she was hesitating, "it's the very least I can do."

"I – it's very kind of you," she acknowledged. "Becky will be delighted."

He smiled at the suggestion. "And you?" he asked. "I suppose I couldn't persuade you to come along?"

Ruth's heart seemed to miss a beat. "I'd love to," she said spontaneously, "but it isn't possible. I couldn't leave Mother on her own."

"You were preparing to leave her with Amos," he pointed out reasonably enough. "I'd guarantee to get you back in time for your evening meal."

"I – don't know."

"Harrogate can be very nice at this time of year," he persuaded.

"I know." She smiled back at him. "We used to do a lot of our shopping there. I loved walking along the Stray, especially in the spring when all the bulbs were out," Ruth said, "but—"

"But what?" Her mother was standing in the open doorway behind them. "Off you go, Ruth," she advised. "You haven't had a real break for weeks and the Harrogate air will do you a power of good. You baked all yesterday afternoon to leave enough food to keep Amos and me alive for a month. You know it can take all morning for Becky's treatment if she has to wait and Mark will get you back in time to pick her up."

It was no use pretending that she didn't want to go and

Ruth stole a last critical glance in the hall mirror as Mark helped Becky into his car. He had already installed the wheelchair in the boot and was waiting when she reached the door.

"Becky will have more room in the back," he said.

Becky's mind was already on her destination.

"The nurses are great," she acknowledged. "I've made friends with them already."

They drove off in the hazy sunshine down the narrow dale with its green fields criss-crossed by their network of stone walls and the rounded hills on either side waking to the touch of the sun. The tiered limestone cliff of the Scar stood out spectacularly, waiting for the promised warmth of the autumn day. There was hardly a cloud in sight, the sky washed clear by early morning rain, and Ruth sat back determined to enjoy herself.

Once or twice she saw Mark smile as Becky chattered away from the back seat and he certainly seemed relaxed as he guided the big car towards the main highway.

When they finally reached the hospital Becky was told that she would have to wait. One of the physiotherapists had been taken ill and a sizeable backlog had built up in the treatment room.

"That means I'll be here for long enough," she said, not too greatly perturbed. "I can have my lunch with Edith in the café so you can have an hour longer in Harrogate."

"Are you sure?" Ruth asked. "I'll stay with you if you like."

"No way," Becky said. "Off you go and do Mother's shopping in Harrogate. I'll be happy enough nattering to Edith over lunch."

It was a side of Becky Ruth hadn't seen before, this apparent willingness to merge into the background and allow someone else to take pride of place.

"We'll pick you up shortly after two," Mark promised. "We won't keep you waiting."

"See you!"

Becky waved them off, turning eagerly to the young nurse who had come to wheel her away in her chair.

"She makes friends so easily," Ruth said as they left the hospital behind. "I wish I was like that. It takes me a long time to get to know people and even then—"

"You have to be absolutely sure before you can really trust them," Mark finished for her.

"It's not quite that," Ruth protested. "It's just that I don't like to be disappointed in people, I suppose."

"It sounds as if you've had a bad experience," he suggested. "Was that it?"

She bit her lip. "I thought I had fallen in love with someone and he let me down," she confessed.

"You weren't absolutely sure about being in love?" he asked, looking round at her flushed face as they sped along the open road.

"How can you be certain?" she challenged. "You build up a picture and it comes out blurred, maybe because you've over-coloured it." She gazed out through the windscreen. "I was very young."

"And that excuses everything?" There was an odd bitterness underlying his words. "Don't tell me you didn't think twice."

"It all happened so quickly." Ruth didn't want to think back to that lonely time after Tony Grantham had told her he 'needed more space' and was going away. Even now she could still feel the pain of it, the realization that she had offered him more than he was prepared to give. "It's over now," she said, "a long time ago."

"You've put it all behind you?" he asked. "How lucky you are."

They drove on in silence, each busy with their separate

132

thoughts, until they reached the outskirts of the lovely old spa. Harrogate was at its best, steeped in a light autumnal haze with the sun just breaking through to tinge the trees along the Stray with orange and gold. There were flowers everywhere, in the neatly planted beds on either side of the roadway and heaped in bright autumnal colours at the roundabouts and in gardens everywhere.

"Where do you want to be?" Mark asked. "I can let you down anywhere."

"I hadn't thought." She had been too busy gazing down into the past, trying to see where she had made a mistake. "Somewhere near Montpelier Place would do."

He considered that for a moment. "Suppose we stay as we are," he suggested. "I won't be more than five minutes at the solicitor's and we can park outside. Otherwise, it is never easy."

She knew about the problem of parking in a busy town and was more than content to stay where she was. Mark drove down towards the Valley Gardens and up on the far side where he drew in before a terraced block which had now been taken over by business houses whose brass plates shone in the sun.

"Five minutes," he said, unfastening his seat belt. "I have only to sign a couple of documents and pick up some papers. I won't be long."

Sitting in the car waiting for his return Ruth had a strange feeling of wellbeing. It wasn't only the fact that she was here in this lovely spa town she had known for most of her life with someone she had come to admire. It went deeper than that. The Mark she had met and resented in the beginning had proved himself to be helpful and kind. There was compassion in him which he sought to hide, but she had glimpsed it in his desire to help Becky and even her mother. She thought about the time when he had carried the sickly lamb down from the high meadow for her and she had recognized tenderness in his touch. Was she trusting too much? That there was a darker side to his nature she was well aware. He could be ruthless when occasion demanded, as she had seen when he had dealt with Tim Spurrier in no uncertain manner. Tim had deserved a reprimand and no doubt he had deserved his instant dismissal, but it certainly proved that Mark would not countenance defiance. She had never met anyone quite so sure of his own integrity before, never come up against a character quite so strong.

When he rejoined her she had got out of the car and was looking down over the Gardens, her thoughts once again in the past.

"Would you like to walk?" he asked. "There's a gate up here and we could go down through the Gardens. The car will be quite safe where it is."

They walked to the gate and past the little green-roofed Pump Room which was now a museum of spa life until they came to the miniature valley where the water garden cascaded in tiny falls down to the lower level of the town.

"This is magic!" Ruth said. "Just the sound of the water and the birds. I'd forgotten how peaceful it was and I've never seen so many flowers. Of course, Harrogate is famous for them, but they seem especially beautiful today."

Mark put his hand under her elbow to guide her through the main gate. "Where can we have lunch?" he asked.

"Surely it isn't that time already?" Ruth glanced at her wrist-watch. "I had no idea it was quarter to twelve."

"If you have to shop it doesn't give you much time," he suggested.

"I can get what I want down here," she decided. "I had no idea it was so late."

He looked about him. "What about The Crown?" he asked. "Is it somewhere you can recommend?"

Ruth had never been in The Crown but she nodded eagerly. "When we came through as a family we were always going to some show or other," she remembered. "We never went to an hotel. My father always believed in eating where there was business to be done, generally in a tent!"

They crossed the road to the hotel, Mark's guiding hand still beneath her elbow as the traffic rushed ahead of them.

"I'll give you half an hour shopping time while I go in and book a table," he said.

Ruth hurried through her shopping. Her mother's list was not long and she wanted very little for herself. On an impulse she bought Becky a silk scarf as well as the cardigan she had requested, coming back satisfied, with half a dozen carrier-bags in her hand, to find Mark waiting for her. Her heart gave a sudden great bound of joy at the sight of him. Quite apart from being the most distinguished-looking man around, he was also her escort. What more could she ask?

"I went up for the car," he said, moving towards the Daimler which was now parked outside the hotel door. "I thought it would save time when we have to be back at the hospital for two o'clock."

Time was running away from her, Ruth thought. Her wonderful day was already half spent.

Over lunch Mark talked about High Parks, what he planned for it as a high-class stud.

"I don't want it to get too big," he said. "It would become impersonal then. It has to be a home as well as a breeding establishment for horses. Having said that, I confess I'm ambitious enough to want a winner or two, but that's not my main aim in life. I'm trying to say that

135

I want security, something rock-solid to build on in the future. The sort of thing my sister has over at the Quarry House, for example." Suddenly his expression changed and a dark, hard look appeared in his eyes. "Maybe I'm expecting too much," he added. "Maybe I'm looking for a pie in the sky."

"I hope not," Ruth said huskily. "I hope everything will turn out right for you."

"I've a long way to go," he decided, the look softening. "I haven't even furnished the house yet. I want to get it right, too. Nothing showy or out of character. Antiques, I suppose I mean."

"The Dales are the right place for that," Ruth assured him. "You couldn't do much better than Tennant's at Layburn or even here, in Harrogate, though you'd pay more here."

"That's what Emma thinks," he acknowledged. "She has excellent taste."

Ruth drew in a swift breath. Emma, she thought. Was he trying to tell her that Emma was already his choice as his future wife? Some of the sunshine went out of her day as she followed him to his car. Emma at High Parks where she had imagined her all along.

It rained on their way back to the hospital, light autumnal rain that clung to the windscreen in little drops like tears, and Mark swished them away with the wipers as if he had no patience with them because he needed a clear view before him.

"What did you buy?" he asked. "All these fancy carrier-bags in the back seat."

She laughed at his interest. "A grey cardigan for my mother and a blue one for Becky, and some wool to knit a waistcoat for Amos during the winter," she obliged.

"Nothing for yourself?"

"A pair of sturdy shoes. I came up from London with a lot of inadequate footwear, but now I think I'm fully equipped."

"That means you intend to stay?" he asked.

"Of course. I'm needed, Mark, and it's what I want to do."

"Do you never think about yourself?" he asked. "The job you had and your full life in London."

"It wasn't all that full," she said. "Looking back, there's far more to do in the Dales."

"What about ambition?" he demanded. "Becky says you worked hard to get to London in the first place."

"Only because there was plenty of us at home."

"Jonathan you mean?"

She nodded. "That's all gone now," she said. "There's only Becky and me left."

He looked down at her, seeing her future at Lovesome Hill. "Is that the ultimate sacrifice you want to make?" he asked.

"I don't see it as a sacrifice, Mark." She turned candid blue eyes towards him. "It's something I have to do. Ideally, Lovesome Hill needs a man about the place, but at the moment I can be second best."

He thought about that for a moment. "Don't work too hard," he said dismissively. "Farm life can grind you down."

When they reached the hospital Becky was waiting for them. "You took your time," she observed ungraciously because the physiotherapy had left her exhausted. "Where did you eat?"

"At The Crown."

Becky whistled. "You don't say! Talk about doing things in style. I hear it has been refurbished and film stars stay there occasionally."

"We didn't see any." Ruth handed over one of the

137

carriers. "I bought you the cardy you wanted – and a scarf to go with it."

"Thanks." Becky peered into the carrier. "Thanks a lot. I see you've chosen blue again."

"It's your colour," Ruth assured her. "Did you want something else?"

"No. Blue will do. It doesn't really matter very much when you're sitting in a wheelchair all day," Becky said.

The mood of depression had passed before they came to Lovesome Hill. As they drew level with the gates of High Parks Mark suggested, "Why not come for tea one afternoon? You could sit in the sun and watch the horses."

"I'd like that," Becky agreed. "Ruth could bring me."

"Therapy?" Ruth asked under her breath as Mark drove on past the Stone Birds.

"In a way," he said equally quietly. "It will get her back to normal, not letting her develop a fear of horses."

"You know she may never ride again," Ruth breathed.

"I'm not prepared to believe that," he said. "Becky's got plenty of guts."

"Did I hear my name being taken in vain?" Becky demanded from the back seat.

"Not entirely in vain," Mark said as he changed gear to go down the hill.

Their invitation to High Parks wasn't taken up for over a week because farm work had to come first. The two prize pigs they kept had developed some sort of fever which meant that they saw more of Chay Oliver than they would have done normally, and immediately afterwards the sow produced seven squealing little piglets who filled the air with their joyous squeeks and Ruth's time with an extra feeding pail. Her new stout shoes came immediately into their own as the rain fell and congealed into mud which eventually demanded stouter footwear.

"Wellies from now on, I suppose," she sighed, meeting Amos in the cobbled yard. "That's winter for you!"

"T'aint winter yet," Amos encouraged her. "We'll be ploughin' out in a day or two, tha'll see!"

They had very little arable land; only a small strip bordering the main road where they grew mangolds and winter wheat. Her father, in his last year, had sown rape, producing a field of pure gold which he decided was hardly worth his bother, and now it was mangolds and winter wheat and barley on the stone field, all of which they were able to sell.

Twice during that time Emma had come to Lovesome Hill bringing Harry with her, which was a great delight to Becky. A strange friendship grew between them and Ruth was gradually drawn into it. In spite of the fact that she was sure Mark and Emma would eventually marry and settle down at High Parks she found much in common with Harry's mother, chatting eagerly with her about London where Emma had lived for some time. Apparently she had known Mark long before her marriage to Vernon Falconer, who had been a very wealthy man. When she spoke about her late husband Emma's eyes would cloud over and once or twice her lips trembled uncontrollably as if her memories were anything but happy ones.

When they eventually took up Mark's invitation to visit High Parks Emma went with them.

"I'm advising Mark about the house," she explained. "A man on his own is never very sure in that respect. In some ways Mark's a perfectionist, wanting everything to be just right," she smiled. "He'll want a lot from his marriage, too."

"He hasn't been married before?" Ruth hazard a guess.

Emma shook her head. "No."

It was all she intended to say on the subject and Ruth took the hint.

Mark was waiting for them when they reached High Parks. The fact that the last time they had been there Becky's life had been in danger was in the forefront of all their minds and he seemed to understand how Ruth felt. Motioning Becky towards the side door where there were no steps to negotiate, he left Emma and her small son to follow in their wake while he walked ahead with Ruth.

"Why didn't you bring your mother?" he asked. "It's a lovely day."

"She's having some sort of conference with Amos, probably about ploughing out the stone field before we get more rain," Ruth explained. "Once a farmer, or a farmer's wife, for that matter, the land comes first."

He nodded, leading the way into a small side hall where a wood fire was burning in a wide, canopied grate.

"I thought we'd have tea in here," he said. "It's warmer than the other parts of the house."

Maybe he was avoiding any pain Becky might feel by being entertained in the room where she had lain so helplessly on her first visit to the house and Ruth thanked him mentally for his thoughtfulness. Again and again she was seeing another side of this man and each time her heart bounded with an odd sort of joy. In many ways they spoke the same language, as their unexpected visit to Harrogate had revealed, and Becky had brought out a quick sense of humour in him which Ruth also appreciated. They laughed easily together, a fact which Emma noticed with a small frown between her brows.

Mark had spread an embroidered cloth on the octagonal table he had drawn close to the fire. "Don't expect a banquet," he warned. "I'm doing this on my own."

"I baked yesterday," Emma said. "I've put the basket in the kitchen."

Mark didn't look too surprised. "You think of everything," he said.

Harry was taking up most of Becky's attention while Emma readjusted the table cloth.

"You had it on the wrong side up," she told Mark. "I embroidered that especially for you."

With a kind of horror Ruth could see that the motif on the piece of linen was a cleverly sketched outline of two eagle-like birds which she could only identify as a replica of the Stone Birds guarding the entrance to Mark's new home. They were hardly the subject for an afternoon teacloth and an uncanny sensation of fear ran down her spine as she remembered the legend.

Of course that was nonsense, she assured herself. Mark wasn't the sort of person to believe in legends or anything so ill-fated which would endanger his future. Automatically she crossed to the table.

"Can I help?" she asked him.

"With the tea?" Smilingly he looked down at her, his eyes kind. "I should have asked in the first place."

Ruth followed him through to the kitchen, a vast beautifully appointed place with fitted units in light oak and copper-bottomed pans stacked on the shelves. Quite obviously they had never been used.

"I'd love a kitchen like this," she said spontaneously. "It dwarfs ours completely. You could almost hold a ball in here!"

"It daunts me," Mark admitted, "but I suppose it could be a woman's paradise. Emma chose the pans for me but they've yet to be used."

He was standing beside the cooker which was housed on an island in the centre of the floor and a shaft of sunlight fell obliquely across his face. The thoughtful look in his eyes sent Ruth's heart beating wildly so that she turned away from their searching gaze.

"Will you switch on the kettle for me and I'll make the tea?" she asked almost nervously. "I see you've gone all electric."

"There's nothing else up here," he said, still regarding her intensely, "but I suppose you're still attached to your Aga. Was life on a farm really what you wanted, Ruth?"

She hesitated for a moment, not looking at him. "I haven't thought about it," she said. "Not deeply, anyway."

He switched on the kettle before he came to stand beside her. "There must be regrets," he said. "You had quite a future before you, Becky tells me."

"Becky is prone to exaggeration," she said huskily. "The London business world will survive quite nicely without Ruth Kendal, I guess."

"That wasn't what I asked." He was so near now that she could have reached up and touched him on the cheek, which she suddenly wanted to do. "I wondered if you were content."

"I've never asked myself that question," Ruth answered truthfully. "It's best if you don't start counting costs. I came home because I was needed, Mark, and that's it – full stop. I don't want to live with regrets."

He turned abruptly away. "They can make a hell out of your life," he said gruffly. "Nobody should be made to live with them."

She moved between him and the window where she could look into his face. "If you want to talk, Mark," she said gently, "I'm here to listen."

He stood looking down at her for a moment longer, a dark impenetrable shadow in his eyes before the mask of indifference slid across his face once more. "Talking isn't the solution," he said, "and I've gone beyond hope. I just wanted to make sure that you are doing the right thing by

142

coming back out of a sense of duty alone. Supposing you were to find that you were no longer needed at Lovesome Hill. Would you go back to London then?"

"And pick up the pieces?" Ruth tried to smile. "I'm not sure, Mark. I love the dale and all it stands for. It's part of me now and I wouldn't want to leave it. I think I'll be at Lovesome Hill for a very long time."

Before he could answer that Emma had come to the kitchen door. "That kettle's taking a long time to boil," she observed, "and you haven't even opened my basket."

Feeling deprived of something she had held out her hand to grasp so eagerly, Ruth turned away from her searching gaze. Emma had come at the wrong moment; she had come to put a spoke in her wheel.

It was difficult to know what Mark had been trying to tell her, but one thing she was sure of was that her errant heart was beating far too swiftly, while every nerve in her body was vitally aware of him.

The tea party wasn't quite the success she had hoped for. There was a tension in the atmosphere which reached out even to Becky, while Harry began nagging to go home to Winterside Grange.

"Beauty will be missing me, Uncle Mark," he declared plaintively. "Will you come tomorrow and say 'Hullo' to him?"

Mark ruffled his fair hair. "Sometime tomorrow," he promised. "Probably in the afternoon."

They drove back to Lovesome Hill in comparative silence, a fact which didn't escape Becky's notice.

"What is it with Emma and you?" she demanded. "Is it Mark?"

Was it so obvious, Ruth wondered; was it so easy to see that she was in love with Mark?

"I haven't quarrelled with Emma, if that's what you mean," she stalled. "We are still good friends."

"Except that you are both in love with Mark. It's as plain as a pikeshaft," Becky declared, "and someone's going to get hurt in the end. I can feel it in my bones."

Ruth walked ahead of her into the house.

"Becky Prophet!" she scorned lightly. "You may be imagining things."

"I hope I am." Becky trundled her chair after her, looking concerned. "I couldn't bear to see you hurt, Ruthie – not after all you've done for me."

Ruth bent to kiss her shining hair. "I'm a big girl now, poppet," she declared. "I can take care of myself."

"Can you?" Becky wondered aloud. "Can you be quite sure of that?"

"As sure as I need to be," Ruth said while it seemed that her heart had turned to stone.

"What kind of day have you had?" was Hester's first question when they joined her in the sitting-room.

"Wonderful," Becky assured her. "Strangely enough I didn't mind going up there one bit. I think Mark was slightly nervous about it in case I reacted badly, but it wasn't like that at all. I had to go. I had to see everything happening as I had always imagined it – the horses and the trainers and all the busy life of a stud which I couldn't share any more, and I had to accept that I would always see it from the sidelines. That hurt a bit," she confessed, "but it's something I can't do anything about. Mark knows that and he thinks I should come to terms with it – sooner rather than later."

"He would be doing it for your own good," Hester said. "I think he knows about that sort of thing. Facing facts, I suppose he would call it, however painful that might be. Which makes him a realist," she added, looking down into the heart of the fire.

"You really ought to have come with us," Ruth said. "He did ask you."

"Happen I should," Hester acknowledged at her Yorkshire best. "Was Emma Falconer there?"

"Who else?" Becky answered. "She seems to be up there most of the time these days helping Mark with the house – advising him about furnishing it and that sort of thing."

"She must have the Grange sorted out to her liking now," Hester decided. "Did you know it really belongs to Mark? He bought it for her when she decided to leave London."

"So that they could be near one another," Becky supposed. "Who told you?"

"Kate," Hester said. "She came over for an hour hoping to see you and stayed for a drink of tea. She says it's common gossip in Derham about Mark being the real owner of the Grange."

"I'll put the car away," Ruth said, her heart heavy in her breast.

Chapter Five

A week after their visit to High Parks Ruth found Becky collapsed in her wheelchair.

"Becky! Becky, what have you done?" Ruth cried, kneeling by her side.

"Nothing—"

"That's not true. You were feeling particularly well this morning," Ruth said. "Were you trying to walk?"

"What of it?" Becky's mood was dark. "I thought I could do it by myself, but I can't."

"You will one day." Ruth straightened the rug around her sister's knees. "You know you had a good report from the physio last week."

"And lots of encouragement from Chay. Oh, yes, I know. Everyone's rooting for me, especially Chay because he thinks we'll be married one day."

"Maybe you will," was all Ruth could think of to say in the circumstances.

Becky sat up in her chair. "Who would want to marry anyone in a wheelchair?" she demanded. "Answer me that if you can," she cried. "I'd be an intolerable burden to them however much they said they loved me. I'm a burden now – a burden to everybody!"

It was Becky at her lowest ebb, when disappointment and frustration had overcome her habitual cheerfulness, and she was near to despair.

In spite of everything Ruth could say the depression

146

lasted well into the afternoon until Emma arrived with Harry on their way back to the Grange from their first ride of the day.

"D'you know something?" Harry asked when they had admired Beauty and found him a sugar lump. "Uncle Mark is going to Ireland and we are going with him."

Ruth, who had brought the sugar out to the yard for the pony, stood as if she had been frozen beside his saddle.

"Ireland?" she repeated, looking at Emma.

"Yes," Emma said. "We're going to buy a horse." She bent forward in the saddle to pat her mount's glossy neck. "This old fellow is being put out to grass at High Parks."

Ruth fed her mount a sugar lump. "I hope you'll have a successful trip," she found herself saying conventionally. "When will you be back?"

"At the end of the week." Emma's expression seemed to be full of satisfaction. "We'll come and see you then."

"You'll get down for a cup of tea?" Ruth offered.

"Not today. Heaps to do!" Emma said. "Keep busy!"

"She seems very sure of herself," Becky observed as mother and son rode away. "I hope they won't stay in Ireland for more than a week," she added. "Harry cheers me up no end."

While Emma bewilders me, Ruth thought. She was going off to Ireland with Mark – and Harry, of course – and she was happily fulfilled.

The week dragged past with the thought of Emma and Mark on the far side of the Irish Sea sharing their love of horses and more besides. If they were indeed lovers what an idyllic holiday this must be for both of them.

By the weekend Amos had ploughed out the stone field and there was little else to do except to attend to the domestic animals and think about the weather.

"It be a fine back end," Amos pointed out. "Happen tha'll get all worked out afore Christmas."

The end of the year, Ruth thought, with Christmas and all it meant almost upon them. In previous years she had always come home for Christmas, but this year it would be different. She would be here to stay, part of Hester's depleted family and her righthand man! She knew that her mother depended on her, taking comfort from that.

The weather was good and they were out most of the day while it lasted. One afternoon as she came back to the house after collecting the day's quota of eggs from the hens she felt that someone was watching her. A car had driven up on the main road just beyond the gate and a man was standing beside it looking towards the house. He was too far away for her to recognize him and no doubt he was only a stranger getting out to stretch his legs after a lengthy drive through the dale. People often looked up at Lovesome Hill wondering, no doubt, what it must be like to live in such a lonely place.

Yet, in her turn, she stood watching this stranger, wondering why he didn't drive away. Instead, he opened the gate and began to walk towards her. He was tall and broad-shouldered, like Mark, but it wasn't Mark, of course. She would have recognized Mark even at that distance.

When he had reached the hay barn the man stopped to look about him and then she knew exactly who he was.

"Jonathan!" she cried, laying down the basket of eggs. "Jonathan!"

Her brother turned before she reached him, a broad smile breaking over his face as he recognized her.

"Ruthie!" He held out both his hands. "It's been a long time."

She reached up to kiss him, knocking off his hat. His hair was turning grey.

"I can't believe it!" she gasped. "I can't believe you've come home."

"Believe it," he said. "I should have come back a long time ago – after I knew that the old man was dead."

"How did you know that?" Ruth asked.

"I found an old newspaper in a library – the *Darlington and Stockton Times*," he explained. "There was the announcement of Dad's death. It kinda hit me for six – Mother being alone and all that – but I didn't know how she would take my return after so many years. Then I thought I would come. Just in case I was needed."

There was the faintest trace of an Australian accent there, but in everything else Jonathan hadn't changed very much. Ruth hugged him to her and pointed him towards the house before she picked up the basket of eggs to follow him.

Already Hester was standing at the door, wondering who their unexpected visitor might be. It was late in the year for a casual holidaymaker coming to the farm asking for milk. Then, suddenly, she recognized her son. She didn't speak. She just dropped her walking-stick and held out her trembling hands and Jonathan went into her arms.

"Mom!" he said, holding her close. "Mom!"

They went into the house side-by-side, the tall young man grown grey before his time and the woman who had awaited his return for so long.

Ruth unpacked the eggs in the kitchen with slow deliberation, giving them time to be alone together. When she finally went through to the sitting-room they were seated at one side of the fireplace holding hands.

Jonathan got up to look out of the window.

"How long, were you in Australia?" Ruth asked.

"Three years. I was on a spread in Queensland at first and then I worked my way down country to Melbourne.

I guess I got lucky up north, but I never felt truly settled. There was always the thought of home in the back of my mind. Eventually I sold out. I had made a lot of money because there wasn't much to spend it on and I wasn't a gambler." He looked about the familiar room, at the firelight playing on the rafters and the sun shining in the garden beyond. "I guess I didn't make friends easily because I always thought about home and what might have been. After a while I knew I had to come back – to England, at least. I found a job in Coventry and it was there I saw the newspaper in the library. It seemed to settle all the arguments in my mind about coming home, but I wasn't sure about being needed."

He met his mother's smiling eyes.

"You should have come a long time ago," Hester told him. "But now you have come we'll not be speaking about it again. You're home and that's all that matters."

Jonathan pressed her hand as he passed her chair.

"Where's Becky?" he asked.

Ruth looked towards her mother. "She's out," she said. "Chay Oliver has taken her to hospital for some treatment."

"Treatment?" Her brother turned to look at her. "Little Becky?"

"She's not 'little Becky' any more," Ruth said. "She's been at university for the past year but – she had an accident. She – fell off a horse."

His concern was immediate. "Not Becky! She could ride better than any of us."

"Well – it happened," Ruth said. "Several months ago. She's – learning to walk again."

"And she will," Hester said quietly. "You'll know not to ask her too often how it happened. She's still sensitive about it."

"I can believe that," Jonathan returned. "I can't think

of Becky other than racing around all over the place doing her own thing in her own way all the time. Even as an infant she was always a bundle of energy. Will she go back to university?"

"We don't know," Ruth told him. "We'll have to make that decision when the time comes."

"Well, I'm back," Jonathan said with something of his old bravado. "That should make a difference. I thought you might need me," he added tentatively.

"Need you?" Hester repeated. "We've needed you ever since you went away, but now you're back for good the whole world has changed."

It was perhaps the most emotional speech she had ever made in all her life and she looked almost ashamed.

When Charles Oliver delivered Becky to the door he recognized Jonathan immediately, rushing to shake him by the hand and attempting to thump him on the back from his inferior height.

"Jon, you old so-and-so!" he cried. "What made you stay away so long?"

"This and that," Jonathan said. "I had a lot to consider." He turned to help Charles with Becky's chair, aware of her utter astonishment. "Hullo!" he said. "Guess who?"

"Of course I know who you are," Becky said. "I hope you've come home for good."

"I guess so," Jonathan said under his breath. "I guess I'm needed here."

"We haven't got a fatted calf," Becky observed, "but we can always put an extra chicken in the oven."

The 'fatted calf' was killed in a big way, however, as Hester invited half the countryside to Lovesome Hill to welcome back her son. It wasn't so much a party as a series of parties with Ruth kept so busy that she was hardly able to think. The joy in her mother's eyes filled her own eyes with happy tears on more than one occassion because they were a family again and Lovesome Hill echoed with their laughter as it had done long ago.

Jonathan was good for Becky. He refused to treat her as an invalid and they did most things together. When Mark finally came to Lovesome Hill fresh from his Ireland visit they hit it off immediately, as Becky described it. They were both more or less the same height with the same squared shoulders and narrow hips and horses were in their blood.

"Do you ride?" Mark asked as they leaned over the paddock rail. "I can let you have a horse any time if you care to use it."

"Becky has told me about High Parks," Jonathan said. "I'd be glad of the opportunity till I can get something of my own."

"You know about Becky?" Mark asked. "About the riding accident."

Jonathan nodded. "Ruth told me. She said you were upset about it."

"Upset? I was livid!" Mark's brows drew together in a dark frown. "And I haven't yet made amends for it – if ever one can."

"It was hardly your fault," Jonathan pointed out, "and you sacked the groom. There wasn't much else you could have done."

"Which doesn't make me feel less guilty."

"I don't think Ruth holds you responsible," Jonathan said.

"She seemed to think I was – at the time." Mark pushed his cap to the back of his head. "She probably still does."

"I haven't asked her," Jonathan said, "but I doubt if she would hold a grudge for long."

It was so easy for the two men to become friends. Jonathan settled into the rhythm of Lovesome Hill without

152

difficulty, relieving Ruth of so many tasks that she had far more time to herself.

Time to think? She was reluctant to do too much thinking, she acknowledged, not wanting to believe what her sensitive heart now told her. Mark and Emma were a couple and Jonathan's return to the dale made her own presence less necessary at Lovesome Hill. She felt less needed, less necessary to the smooth running of her family's fortune and more than once she thought of returning to London.

When she met Emma again she expected to see a change in her, but Emma was much the same. She came to Lovesome Hill a few days after Mark and was introduced to Jonathan.

"Hullo!" Emma said, urging Harry forward. "This is my son. I'm trying to get him to ride with more confidence but I'm not having much success. He's secretly afraid of horses."

"I was a bit like that at his age," Jonathan acknowledged. "They seemed a long way up, but my father was determined I wouldn't let the side down and forced me into the saddle whenever possible."

"Which is a mistake," Emma agreed. "Do you ride now?"

"I've half a notion to buy a horse though Mark has offered to mount me up at High Parks in the meantime," Jonathan explained.

"I've just bought this." Emma caressed her horse's glossy neck. "We brought him back from Ireland a week ago when we were there."

Jonathan helped her down from the saddle, smoothing an expert hand along the horse's glossy flank. "He's a beauty," he said admiringly.

"That's my pony's name," Harry piped up. "Beauty. He used to be called Jet."

"Not Becky's Jet?" Jonathan asked. "I thought I had seen him somewhere before. He's a very quiet little pony."

"Then he won't bolt, will he?" Harry asked anxiously. "I can gallop him but I don't like going too fast."

Jonathan laughed. "Old Jet wouldn't bolt if you asked him to," he declared. "He's very docile – very quiet," he amended, catching Emma's eye. "Are you coming in to see my mother?" he asked.

"That was my idea." Emma handed over her reins. "I also wanted to speak to Ruth."

"She's up at the house. She'll be pleased to see you," Jonathan presumed.

Ruth had already seen Emma riding up with Harry. Normally she would have gone out to greet her visitor, but something kept her standing where she was. She had baked their Christmas cake that morning and a mound of mince pies, which she would put into the freezer when they had cooled, and she hadn't had time to change. Suddenly the immaculate Emma seemed a challenge to her and the thought of Ireland rushed back to her mind. Mark had only been to Lovesome Hill once since their return and Emma not at all until now. What could she possibly want?

Taking off her apron and smoothing her hair at the kitchen mirror, she turned to face her visitor.

"Someone to see you," Jonathan announced, opening the door. "It's Mrs Falconer and Harry."

"Hullo!" Ruth greeted them. "How did your holiday go?"

"It was hardly a holiday." Emma laid down her riding-crop on the kitchen table. "We spent most of it rushing round from one stud to the next because Mark wanted me to have the perfect horse."

"He said you had got what you were looking for."

154

Emma smiled. "Yes, I believe I have," she agreed. "Ireland is the most wonderful country, by the way," she added, "and the Irish are most hospitable. We had a wonderful welcome, but, of course, Mark had been there before and knew a lot of people."

"Emma said she wanted a word with you," Jonathan announced, "so I'll make myself scarce. Harry, would you like to feed the hens?"

Left alone with Emma, Ruth waited for her to speak first.

"I wanted to ask a favour," Emma said. "I know you are generally frightfully busy, but I did think I could ask."

"It depends on what the favour is," Ruth said.

"It's about Mark." Emma sat down unasked on a kitchen chair. "He thinks he should do something for the village – open up High Parks for some sort of function now that he has it furnished more or less to our satisfaction."

The word 'our' stood out between them like an unsheathed sword, etched in letters of fire in Ruth's fertile imagination.

"How do you think I could help?" she found herself asking.

"In so many ways," Emma declared. "You know the dale so well. You know everybody and what would go down best at this time of year."

"Not another barbecue. It would be too cold outside," Ruth said. "A Christmas Fayre, perhaps, although that would hardly be original. What does Mark think?"

"Oh, he's easy. He'll do exactly as we say." Emma allowed herself a smile at the thought. "Men are not really very good at that sort of thing, are they? What do you say, Ruth? I'd love it if you would help."

What could she say? Ruth turned to fill the kettle

to make the obligatory cup of tea. "I'd have to think about it—"

"Please say 'yes'," Emma begged. "I couldn't do it on my own."

"It has to be at High Parks?" Ruth asked, thinking about the Grange.

"'Fraid so," Emma said. "It's a sort of image thing as far as Mark is concerned. He wants people to see that he's interested, that he wants to be part of the dale's life. High Parks has been closed for far too long and he wants to underline the fact that he's here for keeps."

"Surely they know that by now," Ruth said. "He has built up quite a successful business already."

"Maybe it has something to do with that stupid legend," Emma mused. "He could be determined to nip it in the bud whether those stupid eagles, or whatever they are, stay up there on the gateposts or not."

Ruth, who had firmly believed in the legend at one time, laughed at the suggestion. "If I know anything about Mark," she said, "he doesn't believe in legends or fate or anything like that."

Emma's violet eyes met her own. "But do you know Mark?" she asked bluntly. "Sometimes I wonder if even I know him really well."

"You've been friends for a very long time," Ruth pointed out.

"Oh – years and years," Emma agreed. "I should know Mark inside out by now, but sometimes I wonder. He can be as aloof as the Devil when he wants to be. Take my word for it."

She was so confident about Mark, about the way he was and how he wanted his future to be, and Ruth could only imagine them spending that future together.

"I'll see what I can do," she said, trying to keep the reluctance out of her voice, "but maybe it is the right

156

time for a Christmas Fayre. People will buy all kinds of things locally to save them a journey to one of the towns and you'd be surprised at how much talent there is in the dale. You'll have all sorts of offers – paintings and handmade toys and marvellous embroidery, to name only a few."

"That's marvellous!" Emma enthused. "Mark thought the proceeds should go to a local cause – something for the playing fields, perhaps, because that would include just about everyone."

Emma had thought things over very carefully even before she had sought Ruth's advice, but she needed help and she was sure she had come to the right person. The dale was very close to Ruth's heart.

When Jonathan heard of her plans over their cups of tea he wasn't greatly impressed. "You can count me out," he said. "I'm no good at that sort of thing."

"Men generally aren't," Emma told him, "but I'm not asking you to knit or anything like that. What you can do is arrange rides for the children. I've got a pony-trap over at the Grange and Beauty can pull it, but we couldn't let the younger children go off in it alone, even with Beauty between the shafts. You'd have to drive, and when I say I'm not taking 'No' for an answer I mean it! Please, Jonathan," she added enchantingly, "you will help, won't you?"

Men were like putty in her hands, Ruth thought, as Jonathan succumbed immediately.

"If you can't find anyone else," he said, "I'll do it."

Hester, too, was more than willing to help. "I'll bake," she offered, "and look out some of my crocheted blankets. They're fine and warm for a winter's night and they'll sell well. Then there's Nora Sterne who does all those silk flower arrangements. She'd be only too willing to do a few for you. And Alf Patrick would give a carving or two. We've only got to ask."

'You' had turned into 'We', making the whole family involved.

"We'd better meet at the Grange," Emma suggested, "to co-ordinate everything. Then we can have a final meeting at High Parks to decide where everything has to go."

Ruth had been drawn into something she was not too sure about, but she could not opt out now, and when Becky arrived back from her hospital treatment with Chay they were also willing to help.

"It's something we need at this time of year," Chay agreed in his quiet way. "Something apart from gymkhanas and the like. Most folk haven't seen the inside of High Parks and they'll flock up there like swarming bees, mainly out of curiosity."

Emma pounced on him immediately. "Could you do some kind of demonstration?" she wanted to know. "Something like a Pets' Hospital? You'd be good at that. Anyway, I'll put your name down for the committee with Ruth and Jonathan and me. That ought to be enough," she decided. "Unless Becky would like to help."

"What could I do?" Becky wanted to know. "I can't move about without this wretched chair."

"You could print notices and get one or two of the grooms at High Parks to help you put them up," Emma suggested. "Mark is quite willing to let them help."

Becky frowned. "I'll see," she said, not too enthusiastically.

"Don't go to the stables unless you want to," Ruth advised. "The grooms can easily come up to the house."

Becky made no answer, but she started on the notices within a week.

The meeting Emma arranged at Winterside Grange was for a Saturday morning and Jonathan drove them there in his car, because it was larger and roomier than Ruth's two-door coupé.

Once before Ruth had been to the Grange when the former owner had given a children's party many years ago, but it was the first time she had seen Emma in her new home. Winterside Grange stood on an elevated ridge on the far side of the dale with magnificent views across the meandering river to the plateau above Lovesome Hill. Surrounded by its high stone wall it had a sheltered garden where fruit grew in abundance in regimented cordons trimmed into shape recently by the gardener Emma employed. The shrubbery alone would have been a joy to Hester who had opted to stay at home.

"I'll get on with my knitting," she had said. "There isn't much time and I'm not fond of committee meetings, anyway."

Emma met them at the door, gracious and smiling in a wool suit which shrieked *haute couture* even to Becky's inexperienced eyes.

"Everyone has come!" she exclaimed. "How wonderful! We're in the study." She held the door wide open. "Do come in and feel warm!"

Ruth followed her into the hall and on into the small study at the rear of the house overlooking the garden, where a log fire burned in the wide grate and chairs had been placed around it to make them feel comfortable and warm. Paper and pencils were at hand on two occasional tables, evidence that Emma meant business.

"I've drawn up a work schedule that we can discuss immediately, but first of all we'll have something to drink." She turned to Jonathan. "Will you help me with the sherry?" she asked. "And there's coffee for anyone who would prefer it."

Jonathan followed her obediently, obviously glad of

159

something to do, while Becky propelled her chair towards the window.

"Emma is an organizer," she said. "I understand this place was a bit of a shambles before she took it over. Of course, she had Mark's help and that would make a difference."

Chay, who had arrived independently in his own battered old car, nodded. "New blood is good for a place like Derham," he decided. "It often works wonders, provided the incomers don't overdo things or seem to be patronizing."

"I don't think Emma has rushed things," Becky said. "Anyway, I like her."

Emma came back into the room laughing at some joke she had shared with Jonathan. In a way they were two of a kind who had wandered the world and come back to rest in the Dales. Like Mark, Ruth thought, wondering why he wasn't here. Somehow she had expected him to be at the Grange, even though he was not one of Emma's committee.

"Mark couldn't get away," Emma explained, almost as if she had read Ruth's thoughts. "He had an owner this morning who wanted to look at another horse."

Reasonable enough, Ruth thought, so why feel disappointed when he would have come for Emma's sake alone?

Unconsciously she watched Jonathan, seeing that her brother had eyes only for their attractive hostess. For a man of the world, which he now appeared to be, he had fallen very quickly under her spell and Ruth felt angry. This could mean trouble. She did not want to see her brother hurt by love as she had been, yet in some ways she knew that Jonathan could look after himself.

They talked for an hour before Emma excused herself, returning with a trolley laden with lunch-time snacks.

160

There was smoked salmon and various dips which the men explored hungrily, and vol-au-vents with mushrooms, and chicken in a rich, creamy sauce. Becky helped herself eagerly, attended by Chay, while Emma charmed them all.

"Where's Harry?" Becky asked when they were ready to leave. "I thought we'd have a word."

"He's over at High Parks," Emma said. "Mark promised to bring him back this afternoon."

"I thought they might have appeared for lunch," Emma said, "but once they get together time doesn't matter. Mark is working wonders with my son," she added gratefully, "and Harry can't wait to be with him. What will happen when he finally has to go to school I can't imagine. I wanted to ask you about that, Ruth," she added. "He couldn't go as a boarder just yet. That would be too cruel, but neither of us know much about local education."

"There's a perfectly good primary in Derham," Ruth obliged. "I don't think you could do better for Harry. We all started there, and if you did want him to go farther afield when he is eight there's Liberton on the other side of the Pennines. It has a good reputation and it isn't too far away."

"Mark isn't too keen on prep schools," Emma said, her arched brows drawn in perplexity. "He thinks eight is far too young for someone as sensitive as Harry to be away from home. Mark's like a father to him, I have to say, and I'm most grateful, of course, but we have to settle Harry's future before too long. I can't let him run wild in the dale, doing nothing but riding a pony." She glanced across the hearth to where Jonathan was seated. "What do you think, Jon?" she asked.

"Me?" Jonathan looked surprised. "I don't really have

161

an opinion about that sort of thing. I'm a confirmed bachelor, I guess."

"Confirmed?" Emma queried. "Surely not. You must have an opinion, one way or the other."

"Right," said Jonathan. "I think you should send Harry to Derham Primary where he'll be happy for a year or two. Unless, of course, you change your mind about staying at the Grange."

"Why should I want to do that?" Emma said. "Winterside Grange is my home and I'm happy with my life as it is. I've got Harry – and Mark to help look after him. What more could I ask?"

"I can't think," Jonathan said, "but I'm glad you're likely to be a fixture in the dale, at least for a year or two."

It was bewilderingly plain to Ruth that her brother was attracted to his new acquaintance, knowing nothing about Emma's attachment to Mark, but how could she tell him or warn him off? Jonathan was a grown man and he might see her intervention as an intrusion on her part, which would do nothing for their newfound happiness on his return to Lovesome Hill. On the journey back to the farm she decided to let sleeping dogs lie as much for her mother's sake as for her own.

Yet the thought of Mark at Winterside Grange persisted, deepening her own hurt as never before.

At Lovesome Hill there began what Becky called "an orgy of baking" as they prayed for good weather for the Fayre. Boxes and sacks of this and that which were considered highly suitable filled every available space until, on the great day, they were taken up to High Parks to be placed on their appropriate stalls. Ruth had not promised to help at the stud beforehand simply because she felt that she could not face Mark. If he had become a regular visitor at the Grange it only served to underline her opinion that Emma and Mark were lovers and that they would inevitably marry one day.

However, on the day she changed her mind, driving to High Parks alone because Chay had offered to bring Becky and her mother later for the official opening of the Fayre at two o'clock. Glad that the mellow weather was holding, with the sun shining through the morning haze, she turned in between the gateposts where the Stone Birds glared down at her in undisguised hostility, reminding her of her first encounter with Mark on the day of her arrival in the dale. It seemed years and years ago – a lifetime almost – although it was little more than seven months. Seven months to fall in love again with such dire result! She had given quite a lot of thought to her position since Jonathan's return and the fact that her brother was here and was likely to stay made a difference in her own position at Lovesome Hill. Jonathan had taken up his role as head of the family so easily, recognizing how much he was needed now that his father was dead, and that seemed to be some kind of turning point for them all. Her mother's health had improved dramatically since his return and now Hester was walking without the aid of her stick, happy to be able to play her part indoors while her son worked outside. It was Jonathan who had insisted on the help of a 'daily' to make life easier for her because of the extra work involved in looking after him and they had laughed and said it would take more than the efforts of one sixteen-year-old 'daily' just to cook for him. Wendy Kilvington had come to the farm a week ago, a shy, blushing school leaver seeking her first job, accompanied by her mother who had known the Kendals all her life. She was honest and hard-working and she loved animals, so it seemed likely that she would stay with them until she eventually married.

Before she reached the main entrance to the house

163

Ruth drew in a deep breath. She would have to meet Mark time and time again, hiding her love for him as best she could and, mercifully, he would never see how much it cost her.

"Hullo, there!" She heard his voice as soon as she turned off her engine. "You're late."

He had come up behind her from the direction of the stables, tall and handsome in grey corduroy trousers and a thick knitted sweater with a yellow cravat tucked in at his neck. His eyes were almost dove-grey in the early morning light, looking at her with warmth in their depth.

"Has all this gear to be unloaded immediately?" he asked.

"I'm afraid so." She got out of the car, hardly daring to look at him again. "It's all necessary and I'm sorry I'm late. Have I held things up?"

"Not too much. It was just that Emma hasn't arrived yet and nobody knows what's what."

Ruth opened the car boot. "Which means I'd better make a start," she decided, lifting out a cardboard box full of handmade toys.

"Let me help you."

Mark bent over to carry the box which was heavier than she thought and inevitably their fingers touched. The fire that ran through her veins was impossible to describe. It went down and down, touching every fibre of her, burning its way to her heart.

"I can manage," she cried. "I can manage fine, Mark! You needn't wait if you have something else to do."

"What's the matter with you?" he asked, reasonably enough. "You can't carry all this, and I'm here to help. Why make it difficult for us both?"

She had angered him, reminding him of the things she had said when she had held him responsible for

Becky's accident, but now it seemed that there was something more behind the tightening of his jaw and the way his mouth had clamped down on those final words. Desperately she sought to retrieve the situation.

"I don't want to seem difficult," she tried to assure him. "I want this day to be special. We all do. I suppose it's just that I feel tired."

"Yet you are still determined to carry half a dozen heavy boxes up a flight of steps rather than accept my help," he accused her. "That's sick, Ruth, and you know it. You'll have more to do now that Emma hasn't turned up and I'm bound to support you. We can put it like that if you'll feel better about it," he added, turning to mount the steps.

Ruth followed him with the foolish tears she must never shed burning at the back of her eyes. She had picked up two carrier-bags containing Hester's crocheted blankets and they gave her an excuse to look around for a suitable table.

Mark's home had been transformed. Instead of the empty hall she had crossed when her sister had been carried up to High Parks all those weeks ago there were curtains at the high windows, looped back by tapestry ties, and beautiful rugs on the parquet floor. An antique dresser and a heavily carved table were evidently to serve as stalls and there were more tables in an adjoining room. For the first time the house looked lived in. Someone had arranged great banks of flowers – chrysanthemums and lilies from a hothouse – against the walls and there was the distinct sound of laughter from an inner room.

"It looks as if Emma has been busy," Ruth said, laying down the carriers on the nearest table.

"She was here all day yesterday." Mark put the

165

cardboard box on the floor. "She worked till almost midnight on the flowers. Seemingly she had plenty to spare at the Grange."

"They're beautiful!"

What else could she say? Ruth wondered. That she had never been so sure about Emma's role at High Parks until now?

She was not short of assistance as the morning wore on, however. People she knew from Derham and the surrounding dale arrived with gifts of all sorts which might be suitable for a pre-Christmas sale, many of them staying to help without being asked. At eleven o'clock Mark reappeared to stand beside her.

"Down tools!" he ordered. "It's time you had a break. There's coffee and odds and ends in the dining-room if you care to go through."

"Mark – there isn't time," she objected, half against her will. "All these things have to be priced." She indicated the sizeable pile of gifts still at her elbow. "We'll never be ready by two o'clock."

"You will," he said, taking the pen out of her hand. "Trust me!"

She went with him eagerly then across the hall into the long, raftered dining-room where more of Emma's handiwork was in evidence.

"You've worked wonders in a very short time," she remarked. "Is the house completely furnished now?"

He nodded. "Except for the bedrooms and other odds and ends I'm leaving for later. Do you approve of what I've already done?" he asked.

"It's all very much as it should be." Why was he asking her this when he already had Emma's approval? "Emma has perfect taste."

"I guess," he said. "It always shows, doesn't it?"

He led the way across the room to a table which had

166

been roughly set with sandwiches, biscuits and a few misshapen cakes.

"Help yourself," he invited. "You might not get anything else to eat till after the show is over."

"Can I help you?" she asked, picking up a plate.

"By all means. I'm ravenous! But why so conventional, Ruth? I thought we were in this together, you and me, and Emma, of course."

"Yes," she agreed. "Do you know why Emma isn't here?"

"She had to take Harry to the dentist. He was in pain."

"Mark – I'm sorry." Of course, Harry would come first with Emma. "Does that mean they won't be here this afternoon?"

He shook his head, piling sandwiches onto the two plates she held. "They'll be here," he said. "Emma never lets anyone down."

Emma was due to open the Fayre and Ruth heaved a sigh of relief. "We can relax, in that case," she said.

He led the way to a window alcove where they could sit and look down at the activity going on beyond the terrace steps.

"Do you ever relax, Ruth?" he asked. "In some ways you're like Emma. There's no end to your energy when you're working for someone else."

"I don't think of it like that." She sat down on the chintz-covered window seat, making room for him beside her. "I suppose it's just how we are."

"It's how Emma has always been," he reflected. "She gave up a great deal to marry Falconer and he let her down pretty badly in the end."

When she looked round at him his jaw was set in a hard line, his dark brows drawn above the slate-blue eyes, which she imagined held a look of pain.

167

"You know her very well." Her words were little more than a whisper. "Before her marriage?"

"Not long after. You know I'm Harry's godfather?"

"Yes. Becky told me."

"He's a delicate little boy." Mark's expression softened when he spoke of his godson. "We're hoping he'll grow out of it because there's nothing fundamentally wrong. It was just that he decided to put in an appearance before his time. It was a Caesarian operation and Emma nearly died."

"Is that why she left London?" Ruth asked. "For Harry's sake?"

"Partly," Mark agreed. "She always wanted Harry to grow up in the country and London was never really her cup of tea, but Vern was a Londoner and he couldn't see past the West End. It had everything to offer him – success, amusement and a great deal of money. Those were his goals."

They sat in silence for a moment or two.

"What are you going to do now that Jonathan has come home?" Mark asked abruptly. "Will that make a difference?"

Ruth handed him her empty plate. "I'm not sure," she said. "We haven't spoken about it yet, but I know he means to stay. It has made all the difference in the world to my mother. She now believes in miracles."

He got up to bring their coffee, returning with it on a tray. "All hell's let loose in the kitchens," he said, setting down the tray. "To my mind helpers come in two categories; those who criticize and those who really get on with the good work."

"And those that laze their time away!" Ruth laughed. "Mark, I have to go. Thank you for the sandwiches."

She had spent little more than half an hour in his company but it had made her day.

When Emma eventually arrived to open the Fayre she was full of apologies. "I've cheated," she said. "I should have been here to help you all morning but Harry was sick with a toothache and I had to take him to the dentist."

"Mark told me," Ruth said. "Is Harry all right now?"

"He's making the most of his invalid state, shall we say." Emma drew off her gloves. "Jonathan has him at the moment. They're really friendly," she added approvingly.

She was dressed for the occasion in an immaculate suit which looked as if it had been especially tailored for her in a lovely shade which Ruth could only describe as dove-grey, and she wore a hat in the same colour of velvet, the narrow brim underlined with palest mauve which brought out the true colour of her eyes. How beautiful she was, Ruth thought, and how poised as Mark introduced her to the assembled crowd. They looked so right together, standing there on the raised terrace with the backdrop of High Parks behind them, although she could not look at them for long because the sense of hurt within her had grown out of all proportion and her eyes were suddenly misted by tears.

From the opening speeches to the final rush for teas the Fayre was an outstanding success. The whole dale was out to enjoy itself and enjoy itself it did. By four o'clock there was hardly anything left unsold on the stalls and the children had tired Jonathan out, driving them round and round the stable block.

"Never again!" he declared, collapsing into a vacant chair beside Emma. "You ask too much of me!"

"Surely not," she smiled, her violet eyes half-veiled by her long, dark eyelashes. "I suspect you enjoyed every minute of it. I was watching you! Thanks for looking after Harry, by the way. He's forgotten all about his toothache now."

"My pleasure," Jonathan assured her, helping himself to a piece of cake. "Have you eaten?"

"All afternoon!" Emma smiled. "All sorts of people kept waylaying me with plates of sandwiches."

"Which means you won't accept an invitation to dinner." Jonathan looked disappointed.

"Try me!" Emma's eyes were full of laughter. "Sandwiches don't count as a meal. What had you in mind?"

"There's quite a place over at Middleham," Jonathan said. "Mark told me about it. It's only an hour's run, if you can make it."

"Why not, kind sir!" Emma said, taking off her hat. "I owe it to you for looking after Harry all afternoon. What time will you pick me up? Seven o'clock?"

"Seven it is!" Jonathan turned as Ruth came up to join them. "I'm taking Emma out to dinner," he said. "We're going to Middleham."

All afternoon Ruth had been aware of him looking for Emma when he returned with the pony-cart and now it seemed that Emma had been well aware of his interest. Before they had cleared up and were ready to leave she realized with a sinking heart that her brother was fatally attracted to the young widow from Winterside Grange. For better or worse Jonathan's future was firmly in Emma Falconer's delicate white hands.

When Jonathan explained the situation to his mother Hester nodded her approval.

"I like her," she said. "And probably she doesn't get out very much. It must be a lonely life for a young woman over there at the Grange with nothing but a four-year-old boy to take up her attention."

Ruth heard Jonathan returning to Lovesome Hill after midnight, wondering where Mark had spent the evening.

Becky had also been out late, returning with Chay Oliver in a happy state of mind. "Chay has offered to take me to the hospital tomorrow," she informed Ruth. "It's not his turn, but he thought you would like a rest after today."

Thoughtful, thoughtful Chay, but it left Ruth with very little to do. Now that they had cheerful little Wendy coming in every morning to help in the house she had more time to talk to her mother, sharing Hester's hopes for the future.

"I've got you all together again," she said in a rare moment of confidence. "It's all I ever asked. If Jonathan ever wants to marry I hope it's a lass from the Dales. She'd come here, of course, and take over where I leave off. It's been like that for generations, son following father here at Lovesome Hill, but it doesn't mean you won't be wanted, too." She put a gnarled hand on Ruth's arm. "You and Becky," she said.

With thoughts of Emma on her mind, Ruth turned to the window. "Times change, Mother," she said. "It's early days to talk about Jon and the future. He'll find his place in the dale and make new friends. He seems to get on well enough with Mark."

"I'm glad about that," Hester said. "They're much alike." She took up her knitting. "What are you going to do now?"

"Go for a long walk," Ruth decided. "I've things to think about."

"Take the dogs," Hester advised. "They get restless when Amos hasn't got them on the hill."

It was a clear, bright day with a wind from the south and the two collies were in their element, racing ahead of her and turning back expectantly when she failed to keep up with them. She climbed high, right up on to the moor with the fresh wind in her face and a thousand conflicting thoughts in her mind. If things turned out as her mother hoped and Jonathan married in the near future there would be no real need for her at Lovesome Hill. She would be free to go back to London and continue her career.

She stood quite still, looking out across the dale. This lovely valley, where Norsemen had come all these years ago to till the land and give the Dales a name, where monks had found a refuge and built an abbey to the glory of God, and where the ancient race who had first peopled it had lived in peace in the caves they had carved out of the hillside, high up where the sun shone brightest and the snow never lay, was the only home she had ever wanted. How could she leave it? How could she return to a city which would always seem alien to her, and how could she turn away from love and know only despair?

Yet, how could she stay now that love had passed her by and Lovesome Hill had no longer any real need of her?

It was a problem she had to solve for herself, with not even her mother to help her.

The next two weeks passed with amazing speed. In the run up to Christmas there was much to do, with presents to be bought and hidden in the least accessible places, and holly to be gathered from the lanes where it grew in abundance. Becky, with a new light in her eyes, planned their entertainment.

"We ought to give a party," she suggested. "It needn't be very elaborate; just the family and Chay and maybe the Falconers and Mark."

Jonathan had been seeing a lot of Mark, going often to High Parks to ride and possibly meeting Emma there, Ruth thought, wondering if she should challenge him about Emma or let sleeping dogs lie in the hope that his 'fling' with their attractive neighbour was nothing more than that. He worked hard on the farm, suggesting many improvements which he was willing to pay for himself and he looked content.

Becky was proving more mysterious. She made excuses

for Chay to take her to the hospital for her treatment, leaving Ruth with less and less to do.

"Can you spare a couple of hours to go to Derham with me?" Jonathan asked one morning as she cleared away the breakfast dishes. "I've still got a present or two to buy."

"Why not?" Ruth answered. "There are one or two things I want for Becky's party."

They spoke of Becky on the way into the old market town where half the dale seemed to have gathered on similar errands to their own.

"Do you think she's going to get better?" Jonathan asked. "It's such a waste. I can't see her tied to that wretched chair for the rest of her life."

"Becky will make something of it," Ruth said, her eyes grave. "She'll find her own solution."

"Mark has been talking to her about going back to university."

"I don't think she would go back in a wheelchair." Ruth swallowed hard.

"It would be hard for her," Jonathan agreed, "but Becky's got guts. She's more like the old man than any of us. I always thought so."

"We'll have to wait and see." Ruth looked round at him with a loving smile. "How about you?" she asked.

"How about me what?" He pulled up on the cobbled parking lot. "Are you asking me about the future and what I mean to do?"

"Yes."

"Well, for your peace of mind, I mean to stay. I can't tell you any more than that for the moment," Jonathan added, "but I've known for a very long time that I had to come back. I guess this is where I belong and where I'll want to be for the rest of my life."

They sat in the car for a few minutes, deciding where to shop first until, suddenly, Ruth stiffened. A group of

173

youths on motorbikes had stormed into the parking lot, circled it noisily and driven away again, their white safety helmets glistening in the sun.

"What's the matter?" Jonathan asked.

"I – thought I recognized somebody."

"Not in that mob, surely? They looked pretty much alike to me in all that black leather and needless noise. You could have been mistaken," Jonathan suggested.

Ruth knew that she had not been mistaken. One of the riders had removed his helmet to adjust a strap while still straddling his machine, and it was Tim Spurrier. She was as sure of that as she was of the fact that Tim Spurrier could mean trouble.

The day was spoiled for her after that as she wondered what had brought Tim back to the dale. Was it to find Becky? Perhaps not. Perhaps he was just passing through.

She caught a glimpse of the group again an hour later when most of her shopping was done. They were eating an alfresco meal still astride their bikes, with their white helmets dangling from their handlebars and Tim was definitely one of them.

"Let's go home," she said, stuffing the last of her purchases into her shopping bag. "We don't want to be too late."

"What's eating you?" Jonathan asked. "I thought we might have some lunch somewhere."

"Another time," Ruth said. "It's market day and everywhere will be crowded."

"Just as you say." Her brother turned back towards the square. "Are you sure we've got everything?"

"If we haven't we can come again."

Ruth could only think about Tim Spurrier and the damage he had already inflicted on her family when he had so defiantly disobeyed Mark all these weeks ago at

High Parks. They were in enough trouble as it was with Jonathan and Mark both in love with Emma.

"Jon," she said when they were finally settled in the car, "I'm worried about Becky."

"Aren't we all?"

"I don't mean about her present condition," Ruth explained as they drove away. "I've just seen Tim Spurrier back there in the Market Square on a motorbike."

"You can't be sure. They all look alike to me in their leather gear. They could be anyone."

"Not when they take off their helmets."

"You think he spells trouble?"

"I don't know. Becky had a crush on him, we have to remember. If she saw him again or he decided to get in touch with her anything could happen," Ruth said.

Jonathan frowned. "He could just be passing through," he suggested. "Anyway, I don't think Becky would be so foolish. She's got Chay."

"She had Chay when she first got to know Tim," Ruth pointed out.

"She's changed since then," Jonathan said with conviction. "She's not the same Becky we used to know."

"That's true, but I've got a thing about Tim Spurrier," Ruth said. "I think he's trouble."

"Leave him to me," Jonathan returned grimly. "If he comes near Lovesome Hill he'll have me to deal with and, anyway, there's Mark. He's not likely to let a little runt like Spurrier cause further trouble where Becky is concerned. He was pretty mad at the time, I gather, not only about Becky's accident but about the horses. He won't allow anything more to happen in that direction, I'm sure. Stop worrying about something that might never happen. He might only be passing through."

"I hope so," Ruth said, prepared to be reassured.

In the next few days bad luck seemed to dog High

175

Parks. A series of accidents where horses had gone sick baffled Mark, who called in Chay to see what he could do.

"Chay says he can't understand this sickness," Becky informed them on her return from her latest visit to the hospital. "It's something they have eaten, yet Mark swears they have had their usual balanced diet all the time."

"It's them Stone Birds," Amos decided. "They're trouble an' no mistake. It's enough to make a man sell up an' go back to Australia, if you ask me."

Ruth put the same question to Jonathan.

"Go back to Australia?" he repeated. "Not Mark! He's a fighter. He'll find out who is responsible and deal with them as they deserve."

To her dismay Ruth found Tim Spurrier on their doorstep the following morning. "What do you want?" she demanded, a high colour mounting to her cheeks.

"I'm looking for Becky," he said. "I saw her yesterday, but she was in a car with a bloke and just drove past. Where is she?"

"She isn't here," Ruth lied. "And if you take my advice you won't try to contact her again."

"I have to talk to her whatever you say." Tim was truculent. "If you don't want to help me I'll try something else. I'm with another lad on holiday. I'll be here till Christmas, so there's plenty of time."

She watched him go, swaggering down to the field gate where he had left his motorbike.

"Who was that?" Becky wanted to know, wheeling herself into the kitchen.

"It was Tim Spurrier," Ruth told her.

A bright colour stole into Becky's cheeks. "What did he want?" she asked.

"He wanted to speak to you, but I said you weren't here," Ruth confessed.

176

"And why on earth did you do that?" Becky exclaimed. "I could have dealt with him myself."

"Could you?" Ruth asked. "He's got a persuasive tongue in his head."

Becky shrugged. "He's got a thing about Mark sacking him like that," she said, "but he'll get over it."

"If I were you I'd help him over it right away," Ruth advised. "I wouldn't see him again."

"But you're not me," Becky pointed out. "We just don't think alike. Never have. You and Jon are Musgroves, I'm a Kendal, like Father. I know exactly what I want. What is best for me."

During the night the Stone Birds were struck from their pedestals on either side of the High Parks gates and smashed to pieces in the roadside ditch. Whoever had done the damage had fled on foot across the adjacent fields, because there were no tyremarks or footprints on the thin covering of snow which had fallen overnight, coating the entrance to the drive.

Ruth heard the news from Amos who had been up early to gather in some sheep.

"It's a sign," the old shepherd declared knowingly. "Does tha' see? If the Birds are down there be no more luck up there at High Parks for Mr Bradley nor anybody else."

"That's nonsense," Ruth said. "Someone has done this out of spite." Her mind flew to Tim Spurrier. "Mark will deal with it in his own way."

When she told Jonathan what had happened he went straight to High Parks.

"What do you think will happen now?" Becky asked.

"Mark should call in the police," Hester suggested. "This isn't fate or a legend or whatever you like to call it, it's pure, senseless vandalism and it should be nipped in the bud."

Becky looked uneasy. "I wonder what Mark will do," she said.

To her surprise and to the consternation of most of the villagers Mark did nothing, and when Ruth met him at the post-box he shrugged the incident aside.

"The Stone Birds are better where they are if they're going to cause trouble," he said philosophically. "It's the horses I'm worried about. I've two more down sick and it's beating me."

"Chay thought you had found a cure." Ruth wished she had some help to offer. "He said he was hopeful."

Mark's jaw tightened. "Hope seems to be all we've got," he said. "If this runs through the stables I'll have to start all over again and that might not be quite so easy. Of course, I'm insured, but I thought I was at least half-way to my goal." His eyes narrowed even as he looked at her. "I thought I could set up a home and a family at High Parks before another year was out."

She put out a tentative hand to touch his sleeve. "I'm sorry, Mark," she said. "It shouldn't have happened to you."

Fiercely he turned on her. "Well, it has," he said, "and I'll have to live with it. Meanwhile, you'll be going south, I hear. Jonathan thinks you are unsettled at Lovesome Hill. He feels you want to return to London."

"I haven't made up my mind." The words choked back in her throat. "It's early days and I would have been coming back to the dale for Christmas anyway. If – I do go back to London I'll have to find another job."

For a moment he looked as if he might argue with her and then he said, almost complacently, "If there's no more trouble at the stables I'll see you on Christmas Eve. Jonathan invited me," he added for good measure.

The next day Becky went to the hospital for her final treatment before Christmas. Chay took her because he had a call to make in a neighbouring dale anyway, and they were away until the light faded.

When she heard the sound of the returning car at the road end Ruth crossed to the window to look out, watching as the Vauxhall's headlights stabbed the dusk on their way up to the house. They reached the yard and a door banged. In the half-light Chay got out and went round to the passenger side without taking Becky's chair from the boot and Ruth hurried out into the yard to help.

"Chay," she called, rushing forward, "what's wrong?"

"Nothing's wrong!" Becky's voice was high-pitched with excitement. "Watch this!"

She had swung her legs out of the car and was holding firmly onto the door frame as she attempted to rise to her feet.

"Becky!" Ruth cried in alarm. "What are you trying to do?"

"Show you that I can walk," Becky gasped, her effort leaving her breathless. "I wanted it to be a surprise for everybody."

Chay hurried to her side, putting a supporting arm about her shoulders. "Easy does it!" he cautioned. "We don't take unnecessary risks."

"Get my sticks," Becky ordered. "They're on the back seat."

He fumbled for the metal elbow-support sticks while Ruth looked on in utter disbelief as Becky leaned against her to steady herself. Joy and fear mingled in the look she gave her sister until joy was uppermost.

"It's unbelievable!" she cried. "Oh, Becky! Becky, I'm so glad!"

"Now, stand back," Becky said, measuring the distance to the back door. "I want to do this myself."

Chay put a hand on Ruth's arm. "Let her do it," he said. "Let her go in alone. She has practised this for the

179

past three weeks down at the hospital with the physio. It can't do any harm."

Tears of relief were brimming in Ruth's eyes.

"It's unbelievable, Chay," she cried. "A miracle."

"Not altogether," Chay answered prosaically. "She's worked at it. She gave it everything she had and I'm proud of her."

And you love her, Ruth thought. You really love her because your love is part and parcel of all this and Becky really couldn't have done it alone.

"Oh, Chay," she said when she could speak clearly again, "we'll never be able to thank you for everything you've done. This means so much to us all."

"And to me," he said quietly. "It was an agony to see her in that wheelchair."

"What now?" Ruth asked on their way into the house.

"A lot more patience and a gradual strengthening of her spine. It will take weeks, probably months, but if she perseveres and doesn't do anything silly she should be walking again by Easter. That's the specialist's verdict," he added. "Not mine."

They had reached the kitchen now with Becky hobbling determinedly before them on her two sticks, her shoulders amazingly erect.

"I'm in a straight-jacket," she told Ruth. "A sort of iron corset. It's not very comfortable but I don't have to wear it all the time." She looked ahead into the lighted hall. "Hullo, Mother!" she said. "Guess who?"

"Becky!" Hester placed both hands to her mouth, her fingers trembling. "What are you doing?"

"Walking – and waiting for you to kiss me and tell me how wonderful I am!"

Before she had actually finished the sentence she was in her mother's arms, held close against Hester's thankful heart.

180

"It's God's blessing," Hester managed through her tears. "I've had another answer to my prayers."

"Maybe I've prayed a bit, too," Becky confessed. "Chay says I must have done because down at the hospital they are a bit amazed. They helped all they could, but I was determined to do it," she added. "You know me!"

"Never mind who made it possible," Hester said in a choked voice. "You're walking. You're on your two feet again and that's what really counts."

"We're all behind you," Ruth assured her sister huskily. "We'll do this together, Becky."

Becky put her hand into Chay's. "I couldn't have done it without you," she said. "You know that."

He looked uncomfortable. "Of course you could," he said. "It was only a matter of time. All the same," he added diffidently, "you know I'm still here for you whenever you need me."

Becky kissed his cheek. "I guess I know that," she said. "Everybody has been just brilliant and I don't really deserve you all."

Hester led her to the nearest chair. "Sit yourself down," she commanded. "You've been on your feet long enough. I'll get you a cup of tea."

It was Hester's antidote for all their ills and Ruth set out the cups and saucers, trying to keep her hands from shaking because Becky was standing on her feet again.

"It's going to take time," Chay said, "but she'll be walking freely by Easter. It's a bonus, Ruth, whichever way you like to look at it. Surely nothing else can happen to us after this."

Chapter Six

Christmas Day dawned bright and clear with a scattering of snow on the hilltops and a sky so blue that it might have been spring.

As Wendy was at home with her family most of the domestic work fell to Ruth, but she didn't mind. It was the family atmosphere she loved and there was very little to do because most of the preparations had been completed the day before: the turkey stuffed and trussed ready for the oven; the vegetables in separate bowls; the large dining-room, which was only used on special occasions, decorated to Becky's satisfaction; the table laid with Hester's 'christening cloth' and all the places marked with fancy little name tags, although only the family would be there.

At ten o'clock they would drive into Derham for the church service, where they would met their neighbours to pass the time of day and exchange greetings, as they had done ever since Ruth could remember. Then it would be back to Lovesome Hill and the bright, warm kitchen with the turkey cooking in the Aga and the Christmas pudding on the boil.

She thought constantly of Mark, wondering what he would be doing on his first Christmas Day in the dale. Would he come to church or would he be too busy at High Parks even to think of it? Jonathan, who was going up there with increasing regularity, hadn't said one way or the other.

By the time they reached Derham the church was almost full, with only the odd straggler rushing in at the last minute as they sang the opening hymn. It was then that she saw Mark sitting in the Winterside pew with Emma and Harry by his side. Well, he had come and it seemed it was to make some sort of statement about Emma and himself. With Harry sitting between them, his bright head catching the rays from a shaft of sunlight pouring in through the stained-glass window above their heads, they made a lovely couple with their child. The perfect couple. Ruth did not look their way again.

Coming out into the square after the service they lingered for a while in the sunshine until the raucous sound of motorbikes rent the quiet air in a flurry of sound. Two motorcyclists rode into the square, parking beside the lych-gate where Ruth was standing. One of them was Tim Spurrier. He took off his safety helmet and combed his hair, obviously looking for Becky who was several paces behind, walking with Charles.

Ruth turned protectively towards her, but Becky already had the situation in hand. Adjusting her sticks, she walked purposefully ahead with Chay affording Tim no more than a glance.

Ruth heaved a sigh of relief. Mark had come out of the church behind Becky with Emma and Harry by his side and Emma kissed them all.

"Isn't it a glorious day!" she cried. "Not like winter at all."

Mark bent his dark head to place a welcoming kiss on Hester's cheek and Hester smiled at this unexpected show of affection from someone she genuinely admired.

"Happy Christmas," Mark said. "I wondered if I would see you."

Becky lifted her rosy face to be kissed in her turn and because kissing seemed to be in the air Mark turned, at last, to Ruth. He kissed her as he had embraced everyone else, a cold, conventional little kiss that seemed to turn her wayward heart to stone.

What did she expect? She watched as he helped Emma into his car and drove away with Harry waving to them from the back seat.

"Well, now," said Hester, "we'd better get home. We've lots to do."

Because of the bachelor life he lived in the flat above his surgery, Chay had been invited to join them, a privilege which the family enjoyed. He drove Becky back to the farm with a contented smile on his lips and undisguised pleasure in his adoring eyes. He was ten years older than Becky but he was prepared to wait another ten if she would eventually promise to be his wife.

Ruth tried to be happy for her mother's sake, but a small core of hurt lingered inside her all day. She served the vegetables and brought in the gravy while Jonathan carved the turkey, and finally she lit the brandy she had poured over the plum pudding before she carried it triumphantly into the dining-room in a blaze of flickering blue light.

They laughed a lot and exchanged presents and listened to the Queen's speech until Hester finally closed her eyes and fell asleep in her armchair next to the fire.

"Someone has to wash up," Becky pointed out. "We can't leave it till tomorrow, but we really should go for a walk after eating all that food."

"Off you go, then," Ruth encouraged them. "Chay will drive you as far as the moor. I'll wash up."

Jonathan tied Hester's apron around his waist. "You wash, I'll dry," he offered. "I'm quite good at it. I had plenty of practice Down Under."

"Jonathan," Ruth said as she stacked the plates, "you are going to stay?"

"Of course I am going to stay," he answered. "I've got

a very happy future ahead of me, if I'm not mistaken, and that's what I really came back for." He took up the plate Ruth had just washed. "But what about you?" he asked. "I've a feeling you're not as happy as you should be."

"I'm – happy enough," Ruth tried to assure him, "but I feel I should go back to London."

"Is that ambition or just the fact that you might not be needed here?" he asked. "Because if it's a question of need you can set your mind at rest. We still need you, Ruth. We always will. There," he concluded, "that's about the longest and mushiest speech I've ever made, but I do mean it. Whatever happens Lovesome Hill will always be your home."

Ruth could not answer him for the rush of emotion which rose in her throat. She could only stack the plates, blinking the tears from her eyes so that she would not embarrass him further.

At five o'clock Mark appeared on his way home from Winterside Grange. Ruth saw him get out of his car in the yard, hesitating for a moment before she went to meet him. In the searching light of the outside lamp he looked pale and tired.

"Will you come in?" she asked, holding open the door. "Becky and Chay have gone for a walk on the moor and Jonathan went back to Derham, but I'm sure they won't be long."

He hesitated, standing in the full glare of the light as if he was going to change his mind and depart without telling her why he had come.

"I brought these for Becky," he said at last, holding out the parcel he had taken from his car. "They're books we spoke about some time ago."

"Please come in," she said. "It's freezing cold now and Becky won't be long."

In the warmth of the kitchen they seemed very near.

Mark put the parcel of books down on the table between them.

"Have you had a nice day?" he asked conventionally.

"Lovely." Ruth stared down at his gift. "Being all together for the first time in years has meant a lot to my mother, as you can imagine."

"Yet you're not prepared to stay," he said. "Jonathan told me. He said you want to go back to London to get on with your career. Is that true?"

Ruth turned towards the fire. "It's one reason," she said in a strangled whisper. "Now that Jonathan has come home there's not so much need for me any more. I had the makings of a good career in London with the odd visit back to the dale to keep me in touch."

"In touch with what?" he wanted to know, smiling at the domestic picture she made standing there in the firelight. "The fact that you have a family background to pick up whenever you feel the need of it without being too greatly tied?"

"It's not like that at all," she said, turning to face him. "I've lived out my usefulness, Mark, and I'm going back before I become a burden. Jonathan will marry one of these days – that's inevitable – and he will want to bring his wife to Lovesome Hill. It's a family tradition and I won't stand in his way. Think how I would feel if he had to *ask* me to go." Her voice shook a little, but she steadied it determinedly. "I've made up my mind," she declared. "As soon as Becky is well enough I'm going back to London."

"I wish you luck with your choice." He turned to the door. "What more can I say?" He looked across the kitchen to where she stood with her back to the massive oak dresser with the array of shining plates on the narrow racks. "I'll hear from Jon exactly when you're going," he added. "See you sometime, perhaps."

186

The coldness in him – the indifference – seemed to linger in the kitchen long after he had gone, diluting its warmth as it sank into her heart.

When Becky came in she took up the parcel of books with an eager smile. "Mark never forgets," she remarked. "He's about the kindest person I know. Why didn't you ask him to stay?"

Ruth bit her lip to steady it. "Because he was on his way home to High Parks and because he probably had other things to do," she said. "Jonathan says he's a very busy man with a lot of ambitious ideas for the future."

"Did Jon also tell you that they were thinking of going into business together?" Becky asked. "They could run the yard with extra stabling here at Lovesome Hill."

"Or Winterside Grange," Ruth suggested. "There's scope there, too."

"Never thought about that," Becky admitted. "It's early days yet, of course. Mark isn't fully established and Jon's just a beginner. If one of them backed out it could prove disastrous."

"It may never happen," Ruth said, leaving it at that.

The following day was Boxing Day and they each made their separate plans.

"Chay's coming to take me to York," Becky announced. "We could drop you off at Harrogate, if you like, and pick you up on the way back."

"No thanks," Ruth decided. "I'll take Mother for a run in the afternoon if Jonathan wants to go off on his own."

"He's going up to High Parks," Becky informed her. "He's never away from there when he's got a minute to spare. That's if he isn't at the Grange," she added thoughtfully. "Do you think he has got a thing about Emma?"

"I hope not." Ruth had tried not to think about

187

such a complication. "Emma and Mark are an ideal couple."

"Funny you should admit that." Becky gave her an enquiring look. "I thought you and Mark—"

"Well, you thought wrong." Ruth turned away from her inquisitive stare. "One matchmaker in this family is enough."

"You mean Mother? Of course she wants to see you married to Mark or some other eligible bachelor," Becky declared. "Mothers generally do. They want us all to be deliriously happy and marry the right man. It's natural, I suppose."

"Yes," Ruth said, turning away.

Becky and Chay left early, driving off in the old Vauxhall which had been carefully polished for the occasion. They would try to be back before dark, they promised, but, if not, there was no need to panic. Chay was a careful driver and, after all, they weren't going very far.

Jonathan, who had slept late, came down for breakfast at ten o'clock. "I'll be going up to the yard to see Mark," he announced. "I may be there for the best part of the day. He's got two more geldings he wants me to see and one of the owners may be coming across this morning."

"Go and enjoy yourself," Hester encouraged. "There's nothing much to be doing here that Amos can't cope with."

"See you!" Jonathan said as he drove away.

"How about lunch somewhere?" Ruth asked when they were left alone. "We could go as far as the coast if you got ready in time."

"And waste all this good food left over from yesterday?" Hester was forever the provider. "We'll have our lunch here and then get a good book to read. Maybe one of those Mark brought for Becky yesterday."

"If that's what you would rather do," Ruth conceded. "We can go to the coast some other time."

They ate a snack lunch in front of the living-room fire with the two collies stretched out on the hearthrug between them.

"Jonathan doesn't agree to them being in the house so much," Hester mused. "He says it could spoil them for the hill, but they're both eager enough to be off when Amos whistles. Soon they'll be out on the hill all day when the lambs come and we'll be busier than we are now. Come to think about it, it's nearly a year since you came home."

"Nine months," Ruth said, putting down her book. "Mother, I have to go back to London," she announced.

"Back to London?" Hester echoed. "Why would you do that?"

"Because you have Jonathan and Becky with you now and Wendy to help in the kitchen," Ruth said. "You don't really need me."

Hester sat in silence for a moment. "Is that your true reason?" she asked, at last. "Or is there something more, some other, hidden reason that you don't want to talk about?"

"I've fallen in love with Mark." It was almost a relief to admit the fact and Ruth thought that she had never been able to tell her mother a lie. "And he's in love with someone else."

"Who might that be?" Hester's wise old eyes reflected her daughter's pain. "You're thinking it's Emma Falconer, but are you sure?"

"As sure as I need to be."

Hester considered the possibility. "They've known each other for a long time, it seems," she said.

"Far longer than he's known me." There was a sadness in Ruth's voice that she could no longer hide. "So, you

189

see, it would be better for me to go away – to go back to London and try again. I'd come home," she promised, "as often as I could."

"That wouldn't solve your problem," Hester pointed out. "Not altogether. You would be coming back and renewing your love all over again. You wouldn't be giving yourself a chance to forget."

I'll never be able to forget, Ruth thought. Never, as long as I live. This love was part of her, part of the very air she breathed, part of her heart's yearning, and it would stay with her forever. She wondered if her mother had loved her father like this in the beginning.

"I'd bide your time," Hester advised. "She's a widow woman and Mark might have other ideas."

"You must have seen them together," Ruth said. "Mark adores Harry. He'd make him a wonderful stepfather."

"I agree with you there," Hester said, "and he looks like the marrying kind. That yard up there at High Parks needs a woman about the house, but I doubt if he would marry just for that reason." She gazed out of the window. "What's this?" she asked. "There's somebody coming to the door."

Ruth got swiftly to her feet, meeting her brother as he entered the kitchen.

"What's wrong?" she asked. "Jon – is it Mark?

"Not Mark," Jonathan assured her breathlessly. "He's gone up to the Caverns and I've come back to get help."

"What's happened?"

"Two boys have gone potholing up there. They're in trouble. I'll need ropes and a ladder and you'd better telephone the police." Jonathan made a final effort to control his breath. "With all the rain we had in November the Caverns are awash and there's been a fall of rock. Mark thinks the boys could be trapped. When you've phoned the police get some brandy in a flask and some

190

hot milk. We could be up there for a long time. And blankets," he added as he turned back to the door.

Ruth did his bidding with the thought of Mark in the forefront of her mind. The fact that he was up there on the moor with no one to help him so far put urgency into her step as she bundled as many woollen blankets as she could find into the back of her car and filled two flasks with milk which seemed to have taken a lifetime to boil. Hester had found the brandy for her, preparing to join her on the moor.

"You'll have to stay behind," Ruth persuaded. "Someone has to be here when Chay and Becky get back. Send Chay up to help."

"The whole dale will be out in next to no time." Hester laid her coat aside. "I'll make sandwiches."

"Yes," Ruth agreed, not really hearing what she said. "You'd better contact the doctor as well just in case – just in case he is needed."

She had thrown on her own coat and pulled a woollen hat over her ears, suddenly aware of the cold outside. The flasks and the brandy would be enough for the present, she thought, and Chay would bring her mother's sandwiches with him when he followed her to the Caverns. She knew how long these rescue attempts could take.

Unable to put the thought of Mark out of her mind and what could be happening up there on the edge of the moor, she started her car, driving swiftly towards the main road. Why did people attempt to go into the caves when potholing was such a dangerous sport? she wondered, and who could have been so foolish in weather like this when there had been so much rain the month before?

A full moon had come up over the ridge of the hills before she reached the Caverns and she could see the

191

group of men quite clearly. They were gathered at the entrance to the caves where the soft limestone had been eroded over the centuries by water and she could see the beck glistening in the moonlight as it plunged down from the Scar.

Nearby half a dozen cars were parked in an ordered row on the roadside and she pulled in behind Mark's Land Rover, suddenly full of dread. This was wild country thrown up centuries ago to form dramatic faults on the earth's surface and it seemed that it would always remain a challenge to man.

Clutching the flasks and the brandy, she climbed up the gorge past the waterfall formed by the rushing beck as it cascaded over the limestone plateau above until she came to the Caverns. There were six in all, narrow caves carved into the darkness of the rock face where the potholers had been trapped.

Jonathan came to her side.

"Mark?" she asked.

"He's in there." Her brother nodded towards the caves. "We're going down after him as soon as we can get our equipment sorted out. Can you stand by with the others?" He had noticed the flasks in her hands and the brandy. "Good girl," he said. "You've come prepared."

"Is anyone hurt?" Ruth asked. "The potholers?"

"We don't know yet. One lad got out and they're seeing to him over there." He nodded towards the group of men. "He raised the alarm about an hour ago and he's wet and cold so the blankets will help."

"I'll have to go back to the car for them," Ruth said, looking down the road. "I couldn't manage everything in one go. Do you know who the boy is?"

Jonathan hesitated. "This one is a stranger," he said, "but the other one used to work at High Parks. He's the lad Mark sacked a few weeks ago."

"Tim Spurrier," Ruth said beneath her breath.

"Seemingly they came up on motorbikes to take a look at the Caverns." Jonathan drew on a waterproof suit. "They aren't really experienced."

Ruth stood quite still.

"They were in Derham yesterday morning when we came out of church," she remembered. "Becky knew them."

"Yes," Jonathan said, struggling with a boot strap. "She walked right past them." He moved towards the entrance to the caves. "See you!" he said.

Ruth stumbled back down to the road. It was almost as light as day in the rising moonlight and the first stars were dim above her head, but there was a coldness in the air that numbed her fingers and stole into her heart. Why had Tim been so foolish, leading a companion into such danger when he knew so little of the Dales?

Pulling the blankets from her car, she stood for a moment looking up at the great Scar on the earth's crust which had become a challenge to Tim and his companion, thinking about their inexperience and how difficult it might be to rescue Becky's former companion. Not only had he put his own life in danger but he had threatened Mark's into the bargain. Anger flared in her for a moment until she began to wonder about his background, where he had come from. Had he parents to worry about him as she was now worrying about Mark?

It seemed an eternity before she had climbed back to the Caverns. The rescued boy was sitting on a rough boulder a little way apart from the men gathered at the entrance to the caves, a picture of distress as he hugged his arms around himself in an effort to keep warm.

"Put this on." Ruth held out a blanket towards him. "I'll get you something hot to drink."

He appeared to be unable to move.

"You'll be all right," she assured him, wrapping the blanket round his stooped shoulders. "Are you hurt?"

He mumbled something which she took to be "No", shaking his head as he watched her unscrew the top of the flask which served as a cup.

"Was – is Tim a friend of yours?"

Again that scarcely definable "No".

"Can you – do you know anything about him?" She poured some of the hot milk into the top of the flask, lacing it with brandy. "Where he lives and if he has a family," she prompted.

"He comes from down south." The brandy had done the trick. "He lives with a sister and her boyfriend – nobody special, I don't think. But Missus—" He looked up at her appealingly. "I think he's bad hurt. We was all right till we come to where the water was an' Tim tried to force a way through a cleft in the rock. He kinda got stuck an' then the rock gave way. It was sort of soft, like – not hard at all. It just fell away an' Tim went with it. My, it was dark down there!" He shivered. "We should never have done it."

Ruth kept her opinion to herself, aware that their survivor was partly in shock. "Just drink up the rest of the milk and we'll get you down to the road," she urged. "Don't try to go down by yourself," she warned as she turned away.

At the mouth of the caves she saw that Jonathan had already gone in to begin the organized search for Tim and Mark.

"I've got hot milk and brandy if anyone wants it," she offered. "And there will be sandwiches as soon as Chay gets here."

She knew these men, all neighbours who had rushed to the rescue as soon as the first alarm had been raised, stalwart Dalesmen who had seen tragedy before and were always ready to offer their help in an emergency.

The doctor arrived, puffing up the gorge towards them and Ruth drew a quick breath of relief.

"Who's down there?" he asked.

"Mark and Jonathan." Her voice trembled a little. "They went in after one of the lads who used to work at Mark's yard."

"Another adventurer!" the old medic observed, having seen it all before. "Was he experienced?"

"I don't think so." She shook her head. "I think he just wanted to have a go because the caves were there."

"And risk someone else's life in the process," the doctor muttered. "Was he alone?"

"No. The other boy got out. He's over there." Ruth nodded towards the rock where the survivor still sat shivering under the blanket. "He doesn't seem to be hurt – just shocked, but perhaps you could take a look at him just in case."

The doctor looked down at her with a wry smile. "Shock can be a killer even when you think it's over," he said. "I've seen it happen so often. We're always involved in something or other up here," he added, "whether it be an accident about the house, or a fever, or just a baby being born before it's time. I've often thought about getting myself a nice, safe town practice, but it never happened. The Dales got into my blood a long time ago and I had to stay."

As they got into mine, Ruth thought, and I couldn't alter that however much I tried.

Other cars began to arrive down at the road, their headlights seering across the moor and other men climbed up towards the Scar. There was sound now instead of the awful stillness Ruth had first encountered and when, finally, an ambulance arrived, its blue light flashing, she

195

felt partially relieved. At least more professional help was now at hand.

The paramedics came steadily up the hillside, bearing a stretcher each, which caused her further alarm. They expected the worst.

For the best part of an hour they waited, sharing Hester's offer of sandwiches which Chay had brought up. It was really cold now, the men stamping their feet and blowing on their hands while the listeners at the cave mouth shouted back instructions or signalled for extra help.

When hope itself seemed to be diminishing there was a great shout from the caves.

"They're bringing one of them out. They've got some-one!"

It was Tim Spurrier. He was carried out looking bedraggled and very wet.

Ruth knelt beside him as the paramedics laid him on a stretcher.

"He's OK," the ambulance men assured her. "Wet, of course, and feeling bruised, but there's no bones broken."

A flush of recognition sped over Tim's pale face. "I'm sorry," he gulped. "Sorry about the others."

Mark and Jonathan! Ruth could hardly speak.

"They're both down there," one of the paramedics told her. "There was a fall of rock. One of them is trapped."

Which one? Either of them meant a great deal to her. Ruth turned to the mouth of the cave where another of the rescuers had just appeared, covered in white dust.

"We'll need a longer ladder," he announced. "They're right at the back of the last cave and there's no way in except over the top. That last fall of rock has sealed the opening."

Sick and desperate, Ruth knew that she could only

wait. She wasn't equipped to go down there to help to pull whoever had survived to safety and her heart wouldn't let her differentiate between Mark and her brother. If Jonathan should die her mother's life would be devastated when she now believed that she had regained a beloved son; if it was Mark who died down there in the icy darkness she would never be able to forget.

Biting her teeth into her lower lip, she turned towards the stretcher. "We'll get you down to the road," she said. "There's an ambulance waiting."

Tim looked up at her. "I didn't mean this to happen," he said. "Honest, I didn't. We was just exploring the caves when all that rock came down. We couldn't help it when the boss got trapped trying to free us."

She shook her head. "Just – don't say any more," she said. "You're safe now and you'll soon be warm. You're in good hands." She was babbling her reassurance. "It won't be long before you're in hospital."

Tim tried to raise himself on the stretcher. "I'm not going till they get him out," he said. "I'm not going till I'm sure the boss is all right."

"Tim, you haven't any choice. They may need this other stretcher."

Her voice failed and he could see her anguish.

"I'm sorry," he said. "I didn't mean to cause this bother."

"But you did," Ruth accused him, "because you wouldn't take a telling."

Immediately she was sorry because her impassioned outburst would get them nowhere. "Go down to the ambulance," she said quietly. "You'll be more comfortable there."

He left her without another word, recognizing her authority or perhaps her pain. But he did not allow the

197

paramedics to take him to the ambulance, going instead to join his companion on the rocks.

Waiting became the hardest part. Every now and then a voice would surface from the caves, asking for this or that, and someone would hand down another tool or a longer coil of rope. In between the silence seemed to deepen. Then, with a tremendous shout, someone was brought up out of the darkness of the cave. It was Jonathan, staggering a little as he climbed unaided out into the air. Ruth was instantly by his side.

"Mark?" she cried. "Mark!"

Her brother wiped the sandstone dust from his forehead. "He's still down there in the last cave. We can't get him out," he said.

She didn't feel anything while it seemed that the world was standing still.

"We'll try again," Jonathan reassured her, clasping her in his arms. "There must be some way."

White-faced, she proffered the brandy. "Drink this," she said. "You're frozen."

Gulping down the contents of the plastic cup, he turned back to the cave. "We've got about another hour," he said, "before the water rises."

It was an hour Ruth was never to forget, an hour in which time seemed to stand still while all her love flooded to the surface as surely as the water rising in the cavern beneath them.

When, at last, they brought him out she could not believe that it was really Mark, that all her prayers had been finally answered in one brief moment.

"Mark!" she cried, flinging herself down beside the stretcher. "Mark, I love you!"

There was blood on his face and a deep gash at the side of his head, but he opened his eyes to look at her, blue-grey eyes awakening to the first sign of light.

"He's concussed," the ambulanceman said at her elbow. "We have to get him to the hospital."

Mark waved the suggestion aside, albeit feebly. "I'm all right," he said. "Is everybody else out?"

"Yes. Everyone's safe," Ruth convinced him through frozen lips as Tim Spurrier approached them from the rocks.

"About them Stone Birds," he said, looking down at Mark. "It was me who did it, Guv. I broke them up an' flung them in the ditch. I'm sorry."

"Forget about the Birds," Mark said. "I'll get over them. It was the horses I was concerned about. Don't ever come back to the yard, Tim. I can do without that sort of hassle."

"I swear I never touched them horses, Guv," Tim declared, obviously affronted. "Someone was feedin' them weed, but it wasn't me. I wouldn't hurt a dumb animal, Guv. You know that."

"I have to take your word for it," Mark agreed weakly, "but keep away from High Parks all the same if you know what's good for you."

"Maybe I'm learning my lesson," Tim admitted. "I've got another job over against Osterby and I didn't have to have a reference," he added pointedly as he moved away.

Ruth stood beside the stretcher looking down at Mark who had now closed his eyes, having said what had to be said to Tim. He was drifting into unconsciousness again, oblivious of his surroundings as she looked round for the paramedics. It was her brother who came to her side first. Jonathan helped her gently to her feet.

"They've done all they can for him here, Ruth," he said to her, "and he is now in good hands. They'll get him to the hospital in record time and he'll be fine."

He was trying to reassure her and she knew it.

"What about you?" she asked. "Were you there when the rocks fell?"

"Not too near," he said, "but they covered me in dust. Otherwise, I'm all in one piece, thank goodness. We've only got to worry about Mark. The two lads got off scott free. It's generally the way." He bent over the stretcher as the two ambulancemen approached. "Ready for lift-off, old chap," he said close to Mark's ear. "We'll soon have you in hospital where you'll be OK."

Ruth's heart began to pound a merciless tattoo in her breast as she watched Mark being carried away. It was almost more than she could bear to see him lying there so helplessly when she could only remember him as the strong, virile man accustomed to command. Now he looked curiously vulnerable, as if all his strength had been drained away.

"Don't worry," Jonathan said. "He's not the type to go out without a fight. I know Mark."

"You've made friends so quickly," Ruth said. "I'm glad."

"There may be a reason for that," Jonathan mused, "but we won't go into it right now. First things first. We have to get you home."

Chay came over to stand beside them. "Anything more I can do?" he asked. "People are drifting away."

"There isn't much. The police are on the job now, sealing off the caves until they can be sure they are safe again, so I guess we can go home," Jonathan said.

Going home was difficult for Ruth because there was nothing more she could do. She would wait with the others, fearing for Mark's safety, praying for him with her mother and Becky, waiting and waiting for news from the hospital until they were finally told the truth. Jonathan left her at the farm. "I'm going over to the Grange," he volunteered without further explanation. "I'll have to tell Emma."

Of course, Ruth thought. Emma, who was in love with Mark! Jonathan would go there to console her, once he had told her about the accident, Jonathan who had become Mark's good friend. He would help Emma through the trauma of the accident as he had helped her up there at the Caverns in a kindly, brotherly way that Emma would understand.

"Do you want me to come with you?" she asked. "You know – another woman—"

He shook his head. "It would be best if I went alone," he decided. "Emma may want me to take her to the hospital."

"Of course."

Ruth turned away into the house where Becky and her mother were waiting.

"What a panic!" Becky exclaimed. "Chay phoned to say Mark has been taken to hospital. Is he all right?"

"He was conscious when they brought him out," Ruth managed, "but afterwards he – seemed to go into a coma. He recognized Tim Spurrier and spoke to him, but that was all. He just closed his eyes and – and seemed to go to sleep."

"He's tough," Becky said as if to reassure herself as much as Ruth. "He'll pull through. What on earth took Tim Spurrier into the caves?"

"You can ask that question till you're blue in the face," Hester said from her chair by the fire, "and you'll never get a sensible answer. Men – and boys – do those silly things out of a sense of bravado, if you ask me."

"Or maybe it's because they have to," Ruth mused. "It's like climbing a mountain – just because it's there."

"But Mark didn't go into the cave for that reason,"

201

Becky reminded her. "He tried to save someone's life and it was strange that it had to be Tim's."

Wendy appeared at the sitting-room door. "Will I put kettle on, Missus?" she asked. "You'll all be needin' a good strong cuppa tea."

They drank the tea while they waited, tensed, for the telephone to ring, Ruth standing by the window, her mother in her usual chair, and Becky pretending to read. If she felt guilty she did not express her concern although she looked paler than usual, fidgeting with her hair when it fell over her brow.

Just before ten o'clock the telephone bell shrilled out in the hall. Ruth was first to reach the instrument, holding it stiffly in her hand as Jonathan's voice came through.

"We're still here," he said. "We're still at the hospital. Mark's had a thorough examination – x-rays and all that – and they can't find anything wrong."

Ruth let out a long breath of relief. "Can you bring him home?" she asked.

"Tomorrow," Jonathan said. "To Winterside Grange. Emma won't hear of him going anywhere else."

Tensed and curiously hurt, Ruth considered the alternatives. "Emma wouldn't want him to be at High Parks on his own."

"No," Jonathan said. "She's like that – caring for everyone."

And especially those she loved, Ruth thought. "When will you be home?" she asked.

"Towards midnight, I expect." Her brother's familiar voice came across the line as if from a great distance. "Don't wait up."

Minutes after she had replaced the receiver she was still standing there seeing the pattern of the future through dazed eyes. Everything was falling into place: Emma at Winterside until Mark finally took her to High Parks as his wife; her mother and Becky here at the farm with Wendy to look after them while she would be free to return to her career in London whenever she felt inclined to do so. What, then, of Jonathan? For a long time she had known instinctively that he was falling in love with Emma. He spoke of her constantly with a look in his eyes which betrayed his instant attraction to the lovely widow on the far side of the dale, and whenever he could he had sought out her company, including young Harry, until Emma chided him for spoiling her son. They got on well together, all three of them, while Mark seemed more than content with their friendship.

For a moment she felt angry, accusing Emma of playing with fire, although it did not seem in keeping with her gentle nature, but Jonathan had become very dear to her in the past few months and she did not want to see her brother hurt. It was all a tangle which she could not straighten out because she was so much involved.

Becky and her mother were on their feet when she returned to the sitting-room.

"What news?" Becky asked.

"Jonathan's bringing Emma home tonight and he'll go back to the hospital for Mark in the morning. There seems to be nothing seriously wrong. He jarred his back – an impacted spine I think they called it – but he's going to be all right."

"Thank God for that," Hester said. "Is Jonathan taking Emma home to the Grange or are they coming here?" she asked.

"They'll be going to the Grange," Ruth said. "Apparently Emma wants to keep Mark there for a day or two to – to look after him."

Hester gave her daughter an odd look. "She'll do that all right," she said bluntly. "She's the mothering type, but I doubt if he'll stay there over long. If he's fit and able to stand on his own two feet in a couple of days he'll be back at High Parks exercising his horses and getting on with life. He's not the sort to stand still or play the invalid at Winterside while there's work to do elsewhere."

In the morning Jonathan was up earlier than usual. Ruth heard him shouting instructions to Amos as she got out of bed, realizing that he was attempting to get through his morning's duties as quickly as possible in order to set out for the hospital before ten o'clock. Wondering if he had planned to take Emma with him, she opened her window wider.

"Don't worry about doing your chores before you go," she called down to him. "I'll see to them. Are you taking Emma with you?"

He looked up at her, the morning sun glinting on his fair head. "Not this time," he said. "She wants to have everything just right for Mark."

How unassuming he was, Ruth thought, not showing jealousy in any way, although he must be deeply hurt.

"I don't suppose I could help," she offered. "Over at Winterside, I mean."

"I guess Emma will cope." He called a last instruction to Amos who was making for the moor with the two collies. "Emma's an organizer; she'll know exactly what to do. I might not be back before dinner," he added. "Emma has asked me to stay. Sort of added argument against Mark bolting to High Parks at the drop of a hat," he decided with his usual infectious laugh.

Ruth spent the best part of the day wondering about their journey from the hospital. The weather was good for the time of year and the roads would be comparatively free of traffic as they wound their way up the dale. It was January and the holiday crowds had long disappeared, leaving the solitary hillsides to the bleating of sheep and the cry of birds. She thought of the strange Stone Birds lying shattered in the ditch at the entrance to High Parks, hoping that Mark had survived the legend now that he was coming home all in one piece. Surely there could be nothing ahead of him but success and happiness now that he was going to marry Emma and make a home for himself at the stud.

The day dragged on until Jonathan made his appearance at eight o'clock.

"All's well," he assured them jauntily. "Mark has settled in and is obeying orders. Emma's the sort of person that won't take 'No' for an answer. She'll keep him at the Grange until he's really fit to go back to High Parks. There's nothing spoiling up there and I've promised to do what I can to help. By the way," he added, turning to Ruth, "Emma says you can visit at any time – meaning tomorrow, I suppose."

Ruth knew that she could not go to the Grange, however strange it might look. She could not bear to see Mark and Emma together and loving. Not quite yet. The hurt inside her came flooding back whenever she thought of them as lovers and she could no longer stem her tears. In a day or two, in weeks, in a year she might be able to forget, but now was too soon.

When she heard that Mark had returned to High Parks she was amazed.

"We couldn't persuade him," Jonathan said with a characteristic shrug. "He was adamant and I must say he looks fit enough. Emma thought he was mad, of course, but she had to bow to his wishes. He had work to do and that was it."

"Who is looking after him up there?" Becky asked.

"The woman from the village Mark says Mother found for him, and Emma will be going to and fro," Jonathan answered. "We won't desert him in spite of all his declarations of independence."

It was easy to imagine Mark at High Parks going his separate way, Ruth thought, but what of his obvious love for Emma and her child? She had imagined that they would announce their engagement as soon as Mark had left the hospital, but the days passed and there was no official word. Spring was coming nearer, with the lovely dale making its own preparations for Easter, so perhaps they were waiting to announce their engagement then. Emma was giving a party and invited them all to the Grange.

"It's her way of saying thanks for being accepted," Jonathan said.

Ruth longed to ask if Mark was going, but surely that would be taken for granted. She steeled herself to meet him for the first time since the accident at the Caverns, hoping that she would be able to disguise her hurt but knowing only too well that it would be an effort of a lifetime.

When she saw him again he was standing in the pannelled hall of Winterside Grange hanging up a garland on one of the beams.

"You're early," he said casually. "You'll get work to do before the others arrive."

"I – promised Emma I'd help."

Ruth stood looking at him as if she were seeing him for the first time, tall, slim-hipped and incredibly desirable in his conventional clothes with a gaily patterned waistcoat contrasting with his dark jacket in honour of the occasion. The brief smile on his lips remained slightly sardonic, as if to convey some sort of message which she could not fail to understand. Suddenly every pulse in her body seemed to be throbbing with overwhelming desire and she turned from him in an agony of shame. He was Emma's and he was making sure that she knew it.

Jonathan and Emma were clearing the inner hall for

dancing while Harry was rushing round chasing balloons in a vain attempt at bursting them before his mother stopped him.

Emma, in a violet-coloured dress to match her strange, enigmatic eyes, looked more beautiful than ever as she put the finishing touches to her preparations. There was a sort of glow about her that was hard to describe, like something brightly burning inside her longing to be released. She made everyone welcome in her own charming way, even kissing Ruth warmly when they finally met.

"How lovely!" she exclaimed, pressing a fresh, scented cheek to Ruth's. "I hoped you would come early. Jonathan said you would be willing to help."

"There doesn't seem much more to be done," Ruth said. "Even the garlands have been hung."

"Oh, Mark!" Emma laughed. "We thought he would be tall enough to manage without a ladder. He came over this afternoon – probably because it was too dark to do anything at the yard."

As the final guests arrived the party was in full swing. People were meeting old friends they hadn't seen for weeks, strangers were being introduced and everyone was happy. Jonathan seemed to be in his element, renewing the past with old acquaintances, and he had obviously been a gregarious member of the community at such occasions and evidently very well liked. Emma had invited Hester who had come along to 'sit and watch' the dancers. If she watched her only son more than any of the others she did not conceal her interest, especially when he was with Emma.

Mark danced twice with Ruth, holding her closely although he did not attempt a conversation with her. To Ruth it seemed as if they were drifting through a vague dream in which he held her in his arms without being entirely aware of her as she was of him. His aloofness distressed her because she could not put a name to it and twice her steps faltered before the music ceased.

"Tired?" he asked, leading her to a chair. "Or were you just thinking of something else?"

"I was thinking about the future," Ruth had to confess. "What I want to do with the rest of my life."

"Now that Jon has come home?" His grey-blue eyes were quizzical, his eyebrows raised. "I gather that might make a difference."

"It does, in a way. I came back because my mother was so desperately alone," Ruth admitted.

"And now things have changed," he suggested. "With normality restored at Lovesome Hill you are no longer forced to stay in the dale. When do you go back to London?"

"I don't know." Ruth's voice was far from steady. "Soon, I expect."

How could she tell him that she could not bear to stay in the dale after he had married Emma, and how could she go away never to see his face again? Tears dimmed her eyes for a moment as she turned her head away.

There were games to be played, however, and a quiz to answer. Emma's party must go on. At the end of it she saw Mark standing beside Jonathan and presently they shook hands as if to strike a bargain before they parted. She looked at her watch. It was midnight and some of the guests were ready to depart. Chay would take Becky home to Lovesome Hill on his way back to Derham and she would go with her mother and Jonathan while Mark stayed behind with Emma, perhaps even to remain at the Grange overnight.

It all fell into place so easily, she thought, going in search of Hester who had evidently enjoyed herself.

Her mother was nowhere to be seen, however. She was not in the dining-room and the main hall was almost deserted now. Ruth tried the bedroom upstairs which had served as a cloakroom, but that, too, was empty.

Wondering if her mother had returned to the farm with Becky and Chay, she went slowly down the wide oak staircase to stand arrested on the half-landing as she looked down into the hall. A man and a woman were standing there wrapped in each other's arms. It was Jonathan and Emma.

Frozen in disbelief, she watched as they kissed, a slow, lingering kiss which had nothing to do with frivolity, their arms around each other, their bodies close. It was no party kiss, but a strong, demanding embrace which seemed to hold them oblivious to all around them.

Ruth couldn't move. She stood there watching until they sprang apart, laughing into each other's eyes.

"Tomorrow," Jonathan said. "I'll see you again tomorrow."

Emma drifted away towards the kitchens and Jonathan looked up at Ruth with his usual winning smile.

"Now you know," he said, shrugging his broad shoulders. "Wish me luck."

He turned away to find his car as Ruth continued her search for Hester, who came from the direction of the kitchens with a piece of paper in her hand.

"I've got a new recipe from Emma's cook," she said, folding the paper away in her evening bag. "She thinks it's better than mine, but we'll see!"

When they reached Lovesome Hill Becky was already on her way to bed.

"I'm absolutely shattered," she complained. "And I didn't even dance."

"I'll come up with you," Hester said.

Ruth stood between Jonathan and the staircase. "Can we talk?" she asked beneath her breath.

"Now?" he asked.

"Why not?" She was determined to say what she had to say. "It won't take long."

He followed her into the sitting-room where the fire Wendy had lit earlier still burned in the wide grate.

"What's so urgent?" he asked.

"You and Emma." Ruth switched on a light. "Jon, what are you doing? What are you trying to prove?" she demanded.

He looked at her, frankly puzzled. "I didn't think I had to prove anything," he smiled. "Emma and I are in love."

"You can't mean that!"

"I certainly do – and what's so strange about it, anyway? We want to get married," he declared.

She stared at him as if she hadn't really heard what he had said. "How can you when you are both Mark's friend!" she cried. "How can you betray him like this when you know that he is in love with Emma?"

He looked down at her, a half-pitying smile curving his handsome mouth. "My dear girl," he said gently, "you've got the wrong end of the stick. Mark isn't in love with Emma nor she with him. They are friends. Friends of long standing – of a lifetime, I might say. They never were in love – never could be now. Mark was engaged to Emma's sister and Claire ran off with her brother-in-law. It left Emma completely shattered as Harry had just been born and Mark was his godfather. Mark never forgave Claire for what she did, even after she was drowned with Emma's husband in a boating accident on a Scottish loch. His bitterness went very deep, Emma told me, and he could never trust a woman again. Harry's father was a philanderer, of course. One woman wasn't enough for him. He was not like Mark at all." He put his arm about her. "I'm sorry if I've upset you," he said. "I thought you knew."

210

"How could I known?" Ruth asked bleakly. "How could I ever have guessed?"

"Emma has been widowed for nearly five years," Jonathan said, "and Mark has looked after her. It's my turn now. I think she has come to terms with her husband's perfidy, but not Mark. He still feels a measure of bitterness since Falconer was also his friend. They were a foursome – Emma and Falconer, Claire and Mark. There's no accounting for people," he ended flatly.

Ruth turned towards the door, switching off the light so that only the fire illuminated the room. "I'm glad for you, Jon," she said. "I know Emma and you will be happy together."

"All three of us," Jonathan said. "I think I fell in love with Harry almost before I was sure about Emma."

They went up the stairs together into their separate rooms, brother and sister with different thoughts in their hearts.

When her bedroom door was closed Ruth felt utterly alone, battling with the strange feeling that she had come to the end of a long, dark corridor with no real light at the end of it. Her anger and bewilderment with Jonathan was gone, replaced by a genuine feeling of pity for Emma and her tragic past, but there was still the thought of Mark nagging at her heart. Jonathan's explanation of the past had answered a great many questions for her, explaining some of his initial hostility and reservation where all women were concerned, but what of the future? Was he determined to remain a bachelor for ever? The recluse of High Parks until the day he died.

In her mind's eye she could see the lonely road which now stretched out ahead of him, so like the way she would tread when she finally returned to London because she knew that there could be no other love for her from now on.

Tossing and turning in her narrow bed with a strange white light coming through the gap she had left in the curtains, she could not sleep and the more she thought about Mark the more her despair grew. How am I to live without him, she thought; how am I to fill in all my days? She would come back to the dale from time to time – that was inevitable – only to renew her loss, to see Mark, perhaps, or hear of him with an agony of regret in her heart.

Staring at the ceiling, a single tear ran slowly down her cheek. It was the only tear she shed for her life's loving and she brushed it away with a trembling hand. Tomorrow she would tell them that she must go.

Chapter Seven

"Everything's white!" Becky shouted from her bedroom window. "The whole dale is covered in snow."

It had come in the night, great white flakes falling gently and silently to crown the hills and cover the fields in a soft blanket of pristine whiteness, obliterating the narrow dale roads with only the dark ribbon of the river winding beneath the arched bridge in the valley below.

Ruth stood at her sister's bedroom door. She had been up for an hour and had come up to waken the ebullient invalid who had insisted on returning upstairs to her own bedroom the week before.

"I've come to help you dress," she said. "You've overslept."

"I don't need any assistance," Becky declared, turning from the window. "I'm as fit as a fiddle and rarin' to go!"

She had already struggled into a tweed skirt and was pulling a scarlet sweater over her head.

"I'll leave you to it," Ruth agreed, recognizing her need for independence. "Come down when you're ready."

"Where's Mother?" Becky asked.

"In the kitchen counting mince pies in case we have unexpected visitors," Ruth said. "She's invited Emma, by the way, and Harry."

She found her mother in the kitchen half an hour later as Amos followed her through from the yard complaining about the weather.

"Happen we'll have sheep to dig out afore the mornin'," the old shepherd said practically. "I'll be away up there to see what's what."

"You ought to be coming to church," Hester reminded him.

"Oh ay," he said. "Church be fine after A've taken a look at t' sheep, Missus. A'll away now an' tak' dogs wi' me, if you've no objections."

When he had gone Hester motioned Ruth into a chair. "Sit down," she said. "I've something to say to you."

Ruth chose a chair by the fire, sitting on the edge of it with her hands clasped about her knees. In a rare gesture of affection Hester touched her cheek.

"You know we'll be needing you in the dale whatever happens," she said quietly. "You don't need to be heading away for London even if Jon marries and brings Emma Falconer here as his bride."

Taken aback by the unexpected offer, Ruth did not know what to say.

"It's a big house," Hester added. "We could live peaceably enough."

"It wouldn't work," Ruth said, her voice catching on the words. "Even if Emma agreed it just wouldn't work, Mother. A bride is entitled to a home of her own and, anyway, there would be Becky."

"She'll be back at the university before another term is over," Hester said, unable to hide her satisfaction, "but maybe you're right. I should be looking for a place of my own. Maybe a new bungalow somewhere over Derham way. That would be nice."

"So – Jon has spoken about marrying Emma," Ruth said. "Are you pleased?"

"Pleased that he is content in his choice of a wife – yes," Hester agreed. "Sorry that I'm not going to see you happily wed into the bargain."

Ruth looked beyond her out of the window to the snow-covered landscape.

"We'll talk about it later," she said, "but not now. It's time we were getting ready for church."

They drove to the village together in Jonathan's car, Hester in the front seat beside her son, Ruth and Becky in the back.

"Do you remember when we had to walk all the way there and back," Becky said, "because Father believed that cars were for work and not pleasure? It wasn't always snowing, of course, but it could be cold. Blowing a blizzard, in fact, and we would get to the church frozen stiff and never be really warm for the rest of the day."

"It put backbone into you," her mother told her. "None of you ever had a cold or even a sniffle all winter. You were hardened off."

Most of the villagers had gathered at the parish church for the morning service as they had done, year in and year out, as long as most of them could remember, and because it was clear and frosty and bright they lingered in the churchyard to exchange greetings before they went inside for the service itself.

Recognizing people as they went in, Ruth saw Emma at the lych-gate speaking to Jonathan with Harry in the background surreptitiously making a snowball from the cushion of snow on the stone wall behind them. He wouldn't dare throw it, she thought; Emma would kill him!

Emma was dressed in grey with an emerald-green scarf at her throat and a warm fur hat on her head, looking elegant, as usual, but in some way vulnerable. When she came forward she greeted Hester with a hesitant smile.

"My new daughter!" Hester said. "Or soon to be." She held out both hands. "Welcome to the family!"

Emma's smile was suddenly radiant. "That means so

215

much to me, Mrs Kendal," she said quietly as they entered the church.

Before the service started Ruth was conscious of Mark walking down the aisle towards them. He took his seat in a pew across the aisle flanked by two of the young jockeys from the yard and suddenly it seemed that it was right for him to be there. He was part of the dale now, no longer an 'incomer' who had yet to earn his right to become one of them, and somehow she knew that he would be at High Parks for a very long time.

She lost sight of him when they emerged into the morning sunshine again, but she knew that he would be coming to Lovesome Hill and her heart pounded with a new excitement as she drove Jonathan's car home to the farm.

"Of course I invited him," Hester had said. "He's a man on his own. What would you expect?"

There was much to be done in the kitchen to put the finishing touches to their meal, and Becky's high-pitched laughter seemed to gain momentum as one o'clock approached. Chay was there helping her with her chores and she seemed amazingly content. Emma was folding napkins, while Harry and Jonathan were doing something about feeding the dogs.

"I'll take their bowls out to them," Ruth offered. "They've had a busy morning on the moor and they're sure to be ravenous."

Was it an excuse to look for Mark, she wondered, not quite sure that he would actually come.

When the two collies finally had their grateful noses in their separate bowls she heard the Land Rover coming up the approach road, her heartbeats increasing as she went to the open door of the barn to greet him. Mark got down, struggling with the sizeable parcel in the back of the vehicle.

216

"Do you need any help?" she asked.

"I want to smuggle this in without Harry seeing it." Mark turned to look at her, aware of the rising colour in her cheeks. "It's his birthday and I'd like to surprise him."

"That's going to be difficult," Ruth informed him. "He's everywhere!"

"I've bought him a tractor and trailer," Mark informed her with boyish enthusiasm. "Miniature, of course. I saw it in Harrogate a few weeks ago and couldn't resist it. Do you think it will fit the bill?"

"Admirably. I'd go for it myself if I was twenty years younger," Ruth told him. "We can smuggle it in through the sun room."

A warm, happy glow had descended on the farmhouse. Hester had gathered her brood about her and she had never been so content as she looked from one of them to the other and smiled.

When the meal was over and the board games played to everyone's satisfaction Harry was taken home to the Grange sitting proudly beside his new toy. It was long after his usual bedtime and he made no demur, the happiest little boy in all the dale. Jonathan had borrowed Mark's Land Rover to stow the miniature tractor safely in the back.

"You can take my car if I don't get back before midnight," he told Mark as they drove away.

It was after eight o'clock, but they could see the whole length of the dale under its pristine blanket of snow in the pale light of a new moon, and Mark lingered by the door when the others returned to the warmth of the sitting-room.

"Can we walk as far as the gate?" he asked.

"I'd like that." Ruth turned to walk by his side, hugging her woollen jacket close to her chest, her love mirrored

217

in her lustrous eyes. "The dale is wonderful on a night like this."

Mark did not speak till they reached the gate, then, quite suddenly, he said, "I wasn't fully conscious when they carried me out of the Caverns a few weeks ago, but I thought I heard you say you loved me." He turned to face her, his strong profile etched against the backdrop of the hills, his grey eyes suddenly demanding. "Ruth, will you say it again so that I can believe it's true?"

She held out both hands to him, drawing him near, her lips not quite steady as she whispered once more, "Mark, I love you. I always will."

Instantly she was in his arms in a strong, protective embrace as his lips came down against her own, tenderly at first and then possessively, telling her that he would never let her go.

"We belong here," he said, at last. "I knew that from the very beginning when you stood up there beside the Stone Birds and made me wonder who you were."

"I was coming home then," she remembered. "I thought I would never have to go away."

"Home to Lovesome Hill," he corrected her, "but High Parks is waiting for you now, Ruth. Don't make us wait too long."

Looking down across the moonlit dale she knew that they had come a long way in a short time. They were here together, knowing that they belonged.